The Little Girl
Who Was Too Fond
of Matches

The Little Girl
Who Was Too Fond
of Matches

A Novel

Gaétan Soucy

Translated from the French by Sheila Fischman

Arcade Publishing • New York

for Isabelle

FIRST U.S. EDITION 2001

Originally published in Canada by House of Anansi Press Limited

Library of Congress Cataloging-in-Publication Data
Soucy, Gaétan, 1958–
    [Petite fille qui aimait trop les allumettes. English]
    The little girl who was too fond of matches : a novel / Gaétan Soucy.
    p. cm.
    ISBN 978-1-61145-263-1
        I. Title.
PQ3919.2.S655 P4713 2001
843'.914—dc21   2001022669

Published in the United States by Arcade Publishing, Inc., New York
Distributed by Time Warner Trade Publishing

Visit our Web site at www.arcadepub.com

10 9 8 7 6 5 4 3 2 1

EB

PRINTED IN THE UNITED STATES OF AMERICA

The experience of feeling pain is not that a person 'I' has something. I distinguish an intensity, a location, etc in the pain, but not an owner. What sort of a thing would a pain be that no one has? Pain belonging to no one at all? Pain is represented as something we can perceive in the sense in which we perceive a matchbox.

—Ludwig Wittgenstein

I

WE HAD TO TAKE the universe in hand, my brother and I, for one morning just before dawn papa gave up the ghost without a by-your-leave. His mortal remains strained from an anguish of which only the bark remained, his decrees so suddenly turned to dust — everything was lying in state in the bedroom upstairs from which just the day before papa had controlled everything. We needed orders, my brother and I, so as not to crumble into little pieces, they were our mortar. Without papa we didn't know how to do anything. On our own we could scarcely hesitate, exist, fear, suffer.

Actually, lying in state isn't the proper term, if such a thing exists. My brother was the first one up and it was he who certified the event for, as the secretarious that day, I was entitled to take my time getting out of my grassy bed after a night beneath the stars, and no sooner had I taken my seat at the table in front of the book of spells than down the stairs came kid brother. It had been agreed that we were to knock before entering father's bedroom and that, after knocking, we were to wait till father authorized us to enter, as we were forbidden to surprise him during his exercises.

"I knocked on the door," said brother, "and father didn't answer. I waited until . . . until . . . ." From his fob pocket brother took a watch that had lost its hands in days of yore. ". . . until right away, that's it, until exactly right away, and there was still no sign of him."

He kept staring at his blank-faced watch as if he didn't dare look at anything else and I could see fear, fear and astonishment, rising in his face like water in a wineskin. As for me, I had just inscribed the date at the top of the page, the ink was still wet, and I said:

"That's very troubling. But let's consult the scroll and then we'll see."

We scrutinized the twelve articles of the good housekeeping code of behaviour, it's a very pretty document that goes back centuries or more and it has big initial letters and illuminations if I only knew what that means, but of articles that suggested a relationship, even a remote one, with our situation saw I none. I returned the scroll to its dusty box and the box to its cupboard and I said to my brother:

"Go inside! Open the door and go inside! It's possible that father is defunct. But it's also possible that it's only a stoppit."

A long silence. We could hear nothing but the creaking of wood in the walls, because in the kitchen of our earthly abode the wood in the walls is always creaking. Brother shrugged his shoulders and shook his big head.

"What does it all mean? I don't understand it at all." Then he wagged his finger at me ominously: "You listen carefully now. I'll go up but I warn you, if papa is defunct . . . do you understand? If papa is defunct . . ." He went no further. He turned his face away like a dog when it gives up.

"Don't worry," I said. "We'll face the music, you know."

And brother took the plunge. And that was how he learned that papa's door wasn't locked. We knew of course that it wasn't, wasn't locked that is, when we went inside. But if father were on his feet before us, assuming that a being like him slept through the night, he should, we thought, unlock the door when we woke up, for our convenience. Nonetheless, it was revealed to my brother that morning that father must have slept like that because he was naked, his tongue was sticking out and, moreover, he hadn't locked his door. For it was hard to see why, if he hadn't slept through the night and had been faithful to his habits, he should have taken the trouble of stripping bare to expire. Which meant that he must have slept, and slept naked, and that he must have died in those trappings with no solution of continuity, or so I reasoned.

Brother came up to me, pale as bone. "He's all white," he said. "White?" I replied. "What do you mean? What kind of white? Snow white?" Because with papa you had to be ready for anything. Brother thought it over. "You know that pen on the other side of the vegetable garden, not the kennel on the right, the one behind the woodshed. You see what I mean?" "Yes," I said, "on the other side of the chapel, is that what you're getting at?" "If you sprint down the gentle slope behind it, you come to the dried-up stream." All that was quite correct. "And can you picture the stones that are piled up there?" I pictured them. "Well, father is white like them. Exactly that white." "Meaning he's somewhat blue, then," I said, "bluish white." "Yes, that's what he is, bluish white." I inquired about his moustache, what it looked like. My brother gave me a look like an animal that's being beaten and doesn't understand why. "Did papa wear a moustache?" "Yes," I said, "the moustache he asked us to brush once a week." "Father never asked me to brush any moustache." Ah la la. My brother is an abysmal hypocrite, I don't know if I thought to write that down. He sat at the table, haggard, his knees quaking, as if he were about to faint away for a trip to paradise.

"But is he breathing?" I inquired.

Papa had a way of breathing that left no room for doubt. Even when he had a stoppit and was no more animated than a coat-hook, even when his gaze appeared to be frozen forever, you had only to look at his chest — which started out flat, then swelled up like our only toy the frog, achieved a volume you might have thought to be the belly of a dead horse, then took jerky little pauses as it deflated — to know that papa was still of this world, despite the stoppit.

In response to my question, brother shook his head. "Then he's dead," I said. And repeated myself, something I don't often do: "Then he's dead." What was strange was that when I uttered those words, nothing happened. The state of the universe was no worse than usual. Sleeping the same old sleep, everything continued to wear down as if nothing were amiss.

I went over to the window. A thoroughly singular way of starting the day on the wrong foot. This one looked as if it would be rainy, that was our daily bread around here, unless it snowed. Beneath the lowering sky the fields stretched out, mean and poorly maintained. I can still hear myself saying:

"We have to do something. Actually I think we'll have to bury him."

My brother, whose elbows were on the table, dissolved into sobs with a roisterous sound, like when you burst out laughing with your mouth full. I pounded the table, outraged. Abruptly, brother stopped, as if he'd surprised himself. He sat there with his lips pursed, sucking air and blinking, and his face was as red as the time he bit into one of papa's hot peppers.

He came and stood next to me with his face pressed against the windowpane, an old habit of his, indeed that's why the window was so dirty about six feet from the floor. His breath left mist on the window, as will anyone's who hasn't expired. "If we're going to bury him," he said, "we may as well do it right away, before it rains. It wouldn't be fitting to inter papa in the mud." From the back of the meadow, horse was coming towards us, his belly low, his nose bobbing gently.

"But we have to make him a shroud beforehand, we can't

bury papa like that!" And I said over and over, whispering plaintively and striking my forehead slowly against the window frame: "A shroud, a shroud . . ."

Then I went to the door. My brother asked where I was going.

"To the woodshed."

He didn't understand. Look for a shroud in the woodshed?

"I want to see how we're fixed for planks. You," I added, "go and write down what's just happened."

Immediately, the moans and groans of a spoiled brat.

"You're supposed to be the secretarious today!"

"I couldn't come up with the words."

"Words, words! What words?"

Now look, I'd be ready to set fire to the curtains if words ever failed me, but I was pretending not to care in order to force brother to assume, even slightly, the role of scribbler. But brother is a hypocrite or I don't know anything. To cut short the discussion I grabbed the nail jar with mulish determination, my teeth clenched and my brow furrowed, which must surely have reminded him of father, and that made an impression, I believe.

I trotted down the front steps, careful not to set my heels on the rottenest ones, and headed for the woodshed, as promised. The earth was damp, with a smell of mud and roots that stayed in the head the way bad dreams do when I have them. Vapour came out of my mouth, just like that, as if it had nothing to do with me. The countryside was endless and grey and the pine grove that blocked the horizon was the colour of the boiled spinach that was father's usual breakfast. The village was on the other side, apparently, as were the seven seas and the wonders of the world.

I stopped just next to horse. He too was motionless,

watching me. He was so old, so tired, that his round eyes weren't even the same brown colour any more. I don't know whether, elsewhere on earth, there are horses with eyes as blue as those of the valiant knights whose pictures adorn my favourite dictionaries but, well, we're not put here on this earth to get answers, or so it seems. I went closer and put a whack on his nose in memory of father. The animal recoiled, then lowered his huge face. Again I went closer, I patted his rump, I'm not vindictive. Besides, papa and all that, it wasn't his fault, after all. Perhaps I wrote the word animal somewhat rashly, too.

The rust-coloured gum on the woodshed floor was a result of the sawdust and the rain that wells up from the ground and will never end. I hated stepping in it with my boots; it felt as if the earth were clinging to me, sucking me down towards its belly, which is actually a mouth like that of an octopus, and it sucks you in too, like music. It had been a short while, let's say a few days, since I'd been here. A crust of droppings covered the reaper, scrap iron littered the ground all entangled, the plough no longer knew what the hind end of an ox looked like. As for the Fair Punishment, it was in its corner, gathered into its little heap. It hadn't changed much in recent years, and we moved it around very cautiously, trembling when we took it out of its box. It was as if it had attained its maximum degree of distraughtness, and what was left of it wouldn't dilapidate any more, word of honour, it wouldn't move from here for all eternity. Sometimes I would hold it in my arms for days at a time before I put it away. It's quite something, the Fair Punishment, it will surprise the world one day. Inside there was also the glass box, which I'll talk about again in the proper place at the proper time, we can't avoid it. I said here because it's the woodshed, also known as the vault, where I've hidden away to flee the disaster and to write my last will and testament, which you are reading now. I'll be found when I'm found. Unless I run away somewhere else.

Some warped planks were leaning against the back wall, itself made of wood that expected nothing more from anyone. The rest of the enclosure was made of stones oozing moisture. None of the planks seemed usable to me. Don't expect me to make a grave box for papa out of that! Sitting on a flitch I at least made a sort of cross that might do the trick, even if the two planks didn't really rhyme, they were crossed like eyes. I stopped for a few moments to meditate on what we would inscribe on the cross, or whether it would be better to forget about that. What exactly is a flitch?

In spite of my recent bereftment I allowed myself a smile of complicity with myself as I glanced at the picture of the valiant knight who was my favourite, which I'd placed on one of the corners of the plough so I could come here and admire it in silence and in private those times when my brother left me alone and was somewhere on the estate playing with himself. The picture, which I'd torn out of a dictionary, made me think about my favourite story, and since it was my favourite picture I'd put them both together in the secrecy of my imagination. The story must have taken place in the real world somewhere, sometime, you see. In it there was a princess in a tower, prisoner of what you call a mad monk, and there was the handsome knight who came and saved her and carried her off on a steed whose wings were made of glowing coals, if I understood correctly. I could read that story without ever tiring of it, often I projected it inside my bonnet, with so much emotion that I wasn't sure whether I myself was the knight or the princess or the shadow of the tower, or just part of the background for their love, like the grass at the foot of the castle keep, or the smell of wild roses, or the dew-speckled coverlet in which the knight wrapped the transfixed body of his beloved, that's what you call that person. Sometimes, even as I was reading other dictionaries to improve myself, I would realize that instead of reading the ethics of spinoza which I had in hand, I was rereading from the dictionary of my head this story about the princess rescued by her knight which is my very favourite. I'd even gone so far as to try reading it to my brother at night before we fell asleep, but he, as you can imagine, would soon snore like a pig. Everything about my brother disappoints, always, with him dreams are impossible.

And I brought it all back with me, I mean the two planks and also a spade, back to the kitchen of our earthly abode.

Brother hadn't stirred from his chair, he was part of the landscape as they say. He was staring straight ahead, idiotically is the word for it, at the apple core that for three weeks had been hanging on a thread tied to the beam up above, that we'd made a game of eating with our hands crossed behind our backs, it's a sport at which I shine. Every so often brother would blow abstractedly on what was left of the mummified fruit, as dry as a grasshopper carcass, to make it swing. He hadn't scribbled what one might call a single line in the book of spells. You can't leave him on his own.

"There are no respectable planks," I said. "I'll have to fetch a coffin from the village, but in any case here's a cross."

Horse had followed me and he was watching us through the window. Just like him.

"Are there any cents left?"

I don't know what it was about my words but they weren't entering my brother's head. Village, coffin, cents — those uncommon words turned his understanding inside out. He would start to make some movement, abort it, begin to get to his feet, then sit down again. He reminded me of our former dog when papa had made him eat moth-balls with his daily bread, I mean during the first hour afterwards.

God knows why the thought came to me then that, if father could have foreseen such a thing, he would have liked to take some familiar objects with him beneath the earth. Beginning with brother and me, I mused, but that prospect struck me as excessive and distressing. Our turn would come, of course, our turn to expire, and maybe it would be on the same day or close to it, whenever it is extremely uncted if you can say such a thing. For papa's turn, which seemed to have always existed on the horizon, somewhere we had never fig-ured out, represented a kind of command, an appeal issued, if I dare put it this way, from the womb of the earth, just as heretofore all his orders had issued from the bedroom upstairs. I'm telling it the way it seems to me. But that could wait, I mean our turn, for a few days at least, and maybe for weeks or even centuries, for while we knew from a reliable source, through my father, that we were mortal to the core and that nothing here below would endure, papa had never specified how long it would take for our mortal existence to end and for us, for my brother and me, to pass as corpses from the state of apprentice to that of companion.

I opened the cupboard and checked the contents of the purse, emptying it onto the table. There were a dozen iden-tical coins made of some dull metal and they rolled this way and that. I flattened one with my palm. They rolled isn't exactly correct because in fact it rolled — the dozen, that is — like one man, but too bad, I learned my syntax from the duc de saint-simon, not counting my father. There's still something wrong. I'm always confusing my sin-gulars and my plurals, a real salmonagundi. A cat couldn't find his tail in it.

"Do you think there's enough for us to buy papa a pine suit?"

The pine suit was a joke from father, who didn't churn them out by the myriad but used them in the stories he would sometimes relate to us about those who had died during the days of his youth when he was a fine-looking lad. My brother didn't know any better than I did whether we had enough cents, because father never took us with him when he went to the village with horse to buy provisions. He always came back fished off. We didn't like that, he'd distribute whacks.

"He should have taught us the value of money," said my brother.

"These are cents," I retorted. "Our cents must have the same value as those of the villagers."

I neglected to mention it, but of the two of us I'm the more intelligent. My arguments strike like cudgel blows. If my brother were writing these lines, the poverty of thinking would leap to your face and no one would understand a word.

"But we may need a lot more. When papa left he always took along a pouch packed with cents. He had a lot and I think he used to go somewhere now and then to stock up."

"Where is that pouch?" I asked.

But my brother kept repeating: "He should have taught us the value of money." On those few occasions when he's visited by an idea, it doesn't leave his bonnet easily.

I forced him to lend me a hand and we searched the cupboard from head to toe. It contained nothing but rags, crucifixes, and papa's priest clothes from when he was a fine-looking lad, along with the stories of saints from which papa had taught us to read, and which he required us to reread, to transcribe ever since childhood, every day or almost. They had pictures of people with soft beards who went around in sandals in sunlit deserts with vines and palm trees, amid scents of jasmine and sandalwood that almost wafted from the pages of the books. It was papa who had written them, in that microscopic script that today is mine, is ours. He had pasted in the illustrations himself, after he'd wet them with his long ox-tongue, I remember seeing him do it. Many of the stories that were given to us that way were only imperfectly intelligible, though, if that's the right word. They were set in judea, which is in japan or in some unfathomable lands where we assumed father had lived before we were put upon the earth, here in this landscape. In fact we believed for a long time that the stories were his and that he wanted to bequeath them to us as a memory to protect us from disease. If you supposed only that, father would have been capable of doing miraculous things — causing water to gush from a rock, turning beggars into trees, making mice out of stones, and who knows what. But why would he have left those enchanted lands and withdrawn into the empty space of this barren, cloudy countryside that's frozen for six months of the year and has neither olive trees nor sheep? With his sole source of entertainment, his only company, his two thin, daydreamy sons? No, in time that notion came to seem barely plausible. There was also the library, but that I'll talk about later, with its dictionaries of chivalry and its poisons.

"I wonder if father would let us have used these coins," said my brother all at once.

"Would have let us use them," I corrected.

"Same difference. Maybe papa wouldn't have liked it."

"Papa is dead," I said.

"Maybe we should bury them along with."

I rested the spade against the stove and sat at the table, turning the coins over and over in my fingers and shaking my leg. I always shake my foot when I'm angry, it keeps me from using it on the backside of you know who.

IT MUST HAVE BEEN getting close to noon and still nothing had moved. The rain was making strange sounds as it fell, like mew or woof. Horse had taken shelter on the veranda. The stoneloaf stayed on the table and we folded our arms over our soup, bereft of appetite, a rare occurrence with kid brother. Of course the morning hadn't passed in total silence, and we had discussed the remains, demise in general, what would become of us now, the shroud and the pit. It was pretty well decided that we'd wrap papa in a bedsheet and that would be that, we'd have our shroud. There was still the problem of taking action, for which we didn't feel we'd been conceived, that is, going up and getting the body, swaddling it, bringing it downstairs, and all the rest, we couldn't envision how it would end. As for the grave, we hadn't yet made up our minds: we would inter him in the empty vacant lot, but where? Any guessing game is as good as another. My brother said near the ravine, by the pine grove. But, you see, I was more inclined towards the woodshed.

I hasten to add that we weren't the kind to change our minds constantly, not me at any rate, and that we'd have eaten our soup and the stoneloaf even if all appetite had fled, as the hour had come for a snackbar. It was just that, before every meal, papa would make gestures and mutter meditations. Without those rituals, as they're called, eating seemed incongruous to us, even reprehensible, let's go that far, for father must have had his reasons. Take for example. One day, having surprised brother dipping his finger into the pickle jam at an hour when it was not appropriate to take sustenance, father had grabbed the bat, that's what it's called, and batted so hard that brother spent three days in bed bemoaning the fate that had had him born that way, I mean dressed in his future remains. Father cared for him conscientiously, and kisses and affection and humph. And what about me?

The soup was getting cold, it made me wonder why my brother had heated it up. That's typical, he's just like horse. I'd taken our frog from her jar and we watched her pranks with glum concentration. She was the only toy in our possession, or almost, and she didn't know many things. She could walk a distance of eight inches, with her legs spread like my brother's when he wakes with a start, looking distraught because he's peed his pants, then she'd flatten herself in front of us along her full little frog's length, which is rather sad and didn't make us laugh. To comfort her, because a frog's life has its despondencies too, I'll have you know, brother would feed her a dead fly which he'd pull from a window jar that we'd fill to the brim with deceased insects for that purpose. She'd croak too, let's grant her that, the way crows do. But there's nothing as exhausting as idleness, and we had the fait accompli. Fine, I say, we must. "We must what?" replied my brother. Ah la la. With him one always had to sweat buckets over explanations, even draw him a picture!

And so we undertook to bring down father's swaddled corpse and lay it on the kitchen table of our earthly abode. That couldn't be done without difficulty, especially the taking down. The remains were becoming rigid, which gave us something to think about. Putting our hands on them was like touching nothing. If we closed our eyes, as I did just to see, we didn't have the impression that our arms were full of father's flesh, we really had to open them and see him to believe it was actually him. It was also hard to bring his swollen ankles together to get the whole thing through the doorway, it was as if there were a spring that made them fly apart every time. Now for thirty-six moons or more we've had at our disposal a kind of carrot made out of metal or stone, I've never been able to decide which, that attracts nails through the power of magic, and once my brother broke the carrot, and if we brought the two ends back together they'd fling themselves on top of one another through the power of magic, but if for instance we kept the left end in its initial position and turned the right end 180 degrees and tried to bring those two ends together they would push each other apart, again through the power of magic, I don't know if you see what I'm getting at. In any case father's legs repelled each other in the same manner, like the two ends of that magnet, that's what it's called. "Turn him the other way up," my brother said, referring to my father, but I protested. "His attributions will hang down," I argued.

On the staircase, it was the wolf on his prey. I mean, brother lost his footing, papa slipped out of our hands over the banister, and he was off like a piano. Everything happens to us, always, there's no avoiding it. Papa crashed to the kitchen floor vertically with his feet in the air like a rabbit's ears. Something must have broken in his neck because he was standing on the back of his skull, which had never been one of his exercises, as far as I know. His chin was squashed against his chest and he looked like someone trying to free a belch from deep inside. I delivered a clout to my brother's face that my father wouldn't have repudiated, and he pulled himself up as best he could, looking not too proud of himself there in the middle of the staircase. I grabbed him by the ear.

"Now tell me, has he or hasn't he got a moustache?" I said, rubbing his nose in it so to speak.

I'm not a violent man but I have my almighty rages too, and I'll have you know, I dot my i's. And the young man burst into tears, humph.

We elbowed aside the bowls of soup and tipped papa

onto the table. The bowls were quick to fall to the floor. Brother wiped his eyes on his sleeve. The shroud had gaped open when it fell and, since father was dressed like eve, it was as if we were on first-name terms with his balls. They were all soft and chubby, much bigger than brother's, or mine in the days when I still had them, and they hung there on the stiff white body like a bearded baby's face. The sausage had flopped to one side, its mouth agape, looking as if it had been shot. I asked brother if he really believed we came from there, in the manner of calves and piglets. Brother stuck his finger inside the sensitive orifice to see if it could stretch enough to make way for two chicks like us. And the sausage grew and stood up, through the power of magic it became as hard as the thighs it fluttered between like a flag, I'm telling you this the way it appeared to me.

Brother had put his hand on his chest to keep his heart from jumping out. Once he'd recovered his voice, which sometimes abandons us, that's life, he said: "No. I think that what he did was knead us from clay when he arrived here and that we're his final works of wonder."

I covered his attributions with the sheet, for I have my modesty, and my brother said apprehensively:

"Now where are you going?"

I already had my hand on the doorknob. "To the village." Brother started searching all around him. When he thinks, brother looks around, panicky, as if his noggin isn't enough and he has to find ideas in things; I don't guarantee the effectiveness of this method.

"What about baby sister?" he asked suddenly. "What are you doing with her?"

I stared at him without replying.

"I said, what about baby sister?" he repeated, more than a little proud of his nasty brainwave.

It was high time, I sighed, to bring the matter back to the barely cold body of papa, who was no longer there to defend himself. Goaded by allusions, actually by hints that father had dropped, last winter we'd examined from every angle the possibility that we had a sister, a little one, who lived somewhere on the mountain, what do I know. But a baby sister! Us! . . . Yet as we thought about it, it's true that a kind of memory, very vague, came back to us from our childhood. A little girl had once been here among us, imagine our amazement, unless she'd been there forever, who knows? And then she'd gone away like a meteor. Brother went so far as to say that she and I were as alike as bubbles. But were these really recurring memories? Were they not rather a false retrospective illusion resulting from our hypotheses? These so-called memories of a little sister beset my brother in particular. Myself, it's never kept me awake nights, or rarely. I don't let myself be easily bombarded by things I don't like. I turn my back on them, I shrug a shoulder, I flick blood at them.

"It was a dream," I said, my hand still on the doorknob.

To be honest, I thought my brother was simply trying to keep me in the house. So I went on: "Unless you'd rather go to the village yourself?"

And wham. It was a low blow, a punch in the jaw, but what can I say, you have to make the best of things. Staying with papa's remains wouldn't appeal to him, I knew that, but if I had ordered him to go to the village himself he'd have hidden in the attic, I knew that too; of the two of us he is by far the more shy. On another hand, brother and I couldn't leave the remains all by themselves and go off whistling hand in hand to the other side of the pine grove. Afterwards we'd have to put papa in a suitable coffin, and to do that one of us would have to make the sacrifice and rush to the village to exchange something for a grave box.

"I'll go at once," I said then, intrigued nonetheless that father had thought it wise to establish such a disparity between the rational abilities of his two sons.

BEFORE I FAITHFULLY TRANSCRIBE the astonishing things that happened to me in the village, I have to talk about our neighbours, mine and my brother's, who numbered something like four. I exclude from the list of our neighbours those whose flesh existed only on the paper whereon were drawn the words that had given them life, cavaliers, for instance, or mad monks, because there would be too many; I shall consider as our neighbours only those who were endowed with bodies like us, though in many ways those bodies were unlike, as much unlike one another as unlike my brother's and mine, though now that I think of it they were undoubtedly less unlike one another than they are unlike our future remains, just as a green apple and a red apple are more unlike one another than a cucumber — and I repeat, they numbered something on the order of four, all categories considered. As for the people in the village, I had not yet determined whether they might be ranked among our neighbours. I'll exclude the hypothetical little sister too, there are limits after all. Instead of saying neighbour you could say fellow man should it strike your fancy, it's allowed, the difference is infinitesimal.

Here they are, all jumbled together. At the beginning of every season an individual used to pay a visit to my late father, though the phrase pay a visit to is presumptuous since we didn't know if they met elsewhere or otherwise. Brother and I anticipated this neighbour without worrying about him too much, with no useless expenditure of energy, since anticipation can be hard on the nerves, but we knew that he'd come eventually, just as we know that the first snow will fall, and didn't get into a flap over it. One morning we'd see papa make his way towards the field. He'd stop in the very middle, arms crossed, rain pelting down or not, turds could have been falling, and we knew that the visit was going to swoop down on us and we hid away. Just past the pine grove the individual would leave the road and make his way straight to my father, the way a gadfly heads for the only flower in the garden. My father would listen to him without unfolding his arms. And then sometimes he would leave, sometimes father would bring him to the house, in which case we would decamp. They'd go up to the upstairs bedroom, from which just the day before papa had commanded everything, and if my brother and I climbed onto the dripstone to spy on them through the window, it was so we could watch them annotate and sign some pages in big registers that papa would then put away in a trunk before he walked the individual back to the very same place right in the middle of the field and crossed his arms again as he watched him disappear along the road he'd come by, because papa was doing big business. All the same, now and then the individual caught sight of us through the upstairs window, when we weren't alert enough to duck his gaze, or sometimes in the kitchen when we didn't really give a hoot owl if he could see us and when he came back down the stairs, he'd look at us as if we were something incomprehensible that was making him queasy.

Another man also came, much less regularly but more often, accompanied by a young boy who didn't seem to get bigger or older from one time to the next, and from the harsh way he treated him we deduced that the boy was his son. Those two came by cart and papa would go off to meet them by the side of the road, there was no question of their soiling our fields with their dirty boots and we didn't mind telling them so. The sole reason for their presence seemed to be to make father fly into a rage, which happened every time. We didn't like it because afterwards father would distribute whacks. Nevertheless, those were the people who kept papa supplied with hot peppers. He would bring a chock-full basket back to the house, grumbling. That shipment would last him barely a week, on my conscience. Any hot peppers within a radius of a hundred metres and my father stopped living till he'd got to the bottom, when he would roll under the table, sated, a volcano between his lips, it was quite a sight. That man and his son were also the ones who brought the billy goat every year. On occasion, the fellow in question would arrive in his cart without his putative son, that's why I wrote something like four, because the times when he didn't accompany him made us question the times when he had seemed to us to accompany him, maybe the boy was only a dream, anyway, counting him, that would make five neighbours.

The one you'd most want to spend time with, if not the most timely, was called the beggar. Judging by the solicitude my father showed him, he must have been an important somebody with access to sluts and blessed virgins I'll certainly have more to say about later on, as well as miracles up his sleeves, besides that he was mute, he expressed himself through throat sounds, the way dogs do. He also had only one leg, stuck in the very middle like a fool's bauble, and he hopped along this earth like a magpie, propelled by his cane. Father would give him something to drink and a sandwich made from food he'd cooked up, then he would make us sit at the same table, the very same table, and not take a bite, just watch him eat, and sometimes we were hungry too, especially brother, who's greedy. Father would comment on this character in his most solemn voice. Often he had him stand up, take off his coat and his shirt, under which he was as woolly as a sheep that hasn't been shorn for three winters, then he'd pull back the man's lips with one thumb to unveil his gums, which made the beggar chuckle with his mouth full. Or else he would ask him civilly to lie on his back and brother and I would take turns bending over his face, holding back his eyelids with our fingers and examining his pupils, irises, and so forth, to see what a beggar's eyes looked like in their deepest depths, in which papa apparently saw constellations. Then he would make him turn around in front of us on his one heel, making numerous remarks intended to teach us about him without skipping any details. Finally, and this would have been inconceivable with any other neighbour, father would open the door himself and let him go after placing a widow's mite in his hand, believe it or not. And then he made us recite the lesson, threatening us with whacks. We didn't like that. And when snackbar time arrived on those days we'd go away with empty stomachs, by father's express decree, to reflect on mendicancy while we gazed at the toes of our shoes, which caused kid brother to suffer more than I did, because I had my expedients, as you will see, when it came to sustenance.

My next neighbour will be a surprise, people will wonder where I come up with these things or what. We only saw him once and, as fate would have it, it was on one of those days when papa and horse had gone to the village. Now, I can't doubt this one's existence because he spoke to me, he touched me, as true as I'm standing here. I was on the back veranda in my little corner I like so much, surrounded by planks, and I was writing with my dictionaries lying there unopened, spread out all around the pots and kettles, so I hadn't seen him coming. My brother had gone to hide in the attic, too cowardly to warn me, as you might expect, it was a man dressed all in black. He was carrying a little satchel, his sudden appearance made me jump, and he said this amazing thing to me: "Is this mister soissons's house?"

I'd never seen one like that, cross my heart, not even in

my head when I was reading, not even in the illustrations. He was older than us but definitely a lot less old than father, I offer as proof the memory I've kept of him. Nothing about his clothing was torn, not one hair of his short haircut was out of place, there was no dried pickle jam around his mouth, no moustache, nothing. He seemed to me to be streaming with brightness, the way father streamed with water when he came out of the lake in summer. He asked again: "Is this the house of mister soissons, the owner of the mine?"

Now as you may well imagine, I wasn't going to pretend I understood. I made as if I were still writing. But I could feel my lips quivering as if bees were buzzing inside. He came closer, his hand shook my knee.

"Hey! I'm talking to you . . ."

That was too much for me. I hunched my head into my shoulders, brought my legs up to my chest and fell to one side, like an owl suffering an embolism. I looked down at the ground between my fellow man's shoes without seeing anything precise, and my eyes spread. I mean I had the impression that without bulging out of their sockets they were growing bigger and bigger, like the circles you make in the pond when you throw a stone. And my sheets of paper that had slipped into the mud, ah la la . . . My fellow man decided, and a good thing too, not to spend too long on my ashes and stepped aside because I was going to die a natural death if this went on, that was obvious to the naked eye.

Speaking of an eye, I watched him out of the corner of one of mine, unmoving, breathing very quietly, inspired by my friend the praying mantis who was nestled within my folded wrists. The fellow man in question walked around our house and observed the neglected state of the premises, with perplexed grimaces and looks of amazement, as if the sight of the roofs, the outbuildings, the stable, the towers had chilled the blood in his prick. He leaned on the windowsill to cast an eye, another one, on the plank-lined kitchen and then, gazing at his glove, he wiped it with his handkerchief, disgusted. He returned to me, so this torture would never end. He spoke a final word to me but everything inside my bonnet was so dumbfounded and confused that I didn't hear a thing, and then he went away. My god, can it be? I felt a tremendous relaxation in the full dignity of my person, I threw my neck back and exhaled a sigh. Some planks were missing from the wall so that it could go all the way to the roof, and that was where kid brother had stuck his chest and I saw his upside-down face snickering light-heartedly from the safety of the attic. On the days that followed I could hardly sleep, as soon as I lay down or stopped writing my heart would start beating eggs, and when my brother caught me in the middle of a stoppit, he'd point his finger and scoff at me with such jubilation that he had to fondle his crotch like when nature calls and you have to answer: "Ha ha, mister's dreaming about prince charming! Ha ha, he's in love!"

And that drove me into such a frenzy that red tears sprang to my eyes, because what does that mean anyway, in love? I could have flicked blood at him. And that's it for our neighbours, whom I'll soon have more to say about and you'll see why.

On summer mornings when he had an urge to pit himself against the lake, papa would first check the temperature with the tip of his toe, the way bears do, before diving in, and I made nearly the same move when I tested the rut in the road with the toe of my boot before setting out along it for the first time in my life, but the ground didn't yield, the earth seemed able to support me there too, and I left without looking back, may god preserve my brother. Horse followed. There was no question of my mounting him because of the sensations I'd experience, and because father would disapprove if he were still on this side of the world, I'm sure of it. For that matter, over the years horse had got closer and closer to the ground, and if I had mounted him his belly would have been scraped by the rough parts of the road and I don't like to see animals suffer for no reason.

That reminds me of a thing my brother did one time, poor birds. You can think what you want about partridges but you have to try to understand them. Brother had captured four or five of them, I don't know how he'd gone about it or what. Be that as it may, he had painted them with essence of turpentine, if my memory for that kind of word is correct, and after giving them a prior caress with the flame of a match he let them loose into the countryside one by one, you see it's as if the only thing my brother thinks about is causing pain. The partridges, what can I say, they panicked, it's only human. They took off pretty damn fast and in single file knocked themselves senseless against the windows of the chapel, to put an end to the torture and their distress at seeing themselves in such fiery trappings, and I'd have done the same, guaranteed. As for papa, when he found out about this act of fucking cowardice you can imagine what he served my brother by way of a homemade thrashing, because it turned out that father had a holy terror of fires, I don't know if it's passed through my bonnet to write that down. But that day's whacks, ah la la, poor kid brother. Stretched out in his birthday suit as if defunct. It's all ancient history now, like everything else on this blasted planet.

I entered the pine grove. I didn't experience the fear I might have legitimately expected, it was weirder than that, I felt as if horse's breath were propelling me forward, strange isn't it, and at the same time I was dreading some exceptional phenomenon — the sky bursting open and depositing at my feet a blast of lightning that would keep me from proceeding farther; or suddenly encountering, at any turn in the road, a precipice seething with tremendous purple smoke — but nothing like that happened and I continued to advance, thinking, to hell with it. I was also struck by the confusion of odours. They rose up suddenly from god knows where, and I jumped, because I always jump when an unexpected perfume nips my nostril, like the time when I dozed off over my dictionaries and then jumped onto my legs because under my nose brother was sticking his two fingers he'd just coated with the ooze from his sausage and then he ran away laughing, and I raced after him flicking blood and calling him false brother. But along the edge of the pine grove, among the wild roses, there were pleasant odours, as if a fairy were amusing herself in surprising me by taking perfumes from her bag of wonders, the way petals are scattered where a prince will walk. Which struck me as a good omen.

And at the same time it left me feeling bereft, for nothing is unalloyed beneath the salt of heaven. I had never left our estate since I was old enough to remember what was happening to me, and such abstinence should have brought me more astonishments, it seemed to me, but aside from the perfumes I've mentioned there was no solution of continuity, I was walking in a space that caught up with me at every step, and for the first time I understood something that heretofore I'd only sensed thanks to my dictionaries — namely that the earth is round like an onion. Had I spied our house, which I'd just left behind, at the far end of the road, I would hardly have been surprised. I'd brought along the spade in case I had to defend myself against serpents or lions, just imagine, and it made the same scraping sound as I dragged it along the road beside me as if it had been sliding across the pebbles three steps from our front stoop, it's hardly worth the trouble of going on a trip, I told myself.

But so it goes. I'd had the perfectly respectable idea of providing us with a rope, which I'd wrapped around horse like a girth, and because of the weight of his belly, which I've mentioned before, it formed two little concave bulges of worn flesh, with the end of the rope hanging down like a prick. Once the coffin had been purchased I could simply attach it to this rope and then horse could tow it along behind him like a toboggan, giving me all the time I needed to frolic in the spinach at will, hey ho! he's no fool, our secretarious. And then all at once the village appeared on my left behind a veil of trees, and I was so stunned that I came to a halt and horse, whose mind was in the clouds, plastered his warm nose between my shoulder blades, for he walks with his head down, as do beasts that have seen all there is to see on this planet and have gotten over it.

Stunned because nothing about the village conformed to what I'd imagined, and what it was was unimaginable, I'd expected a palace with a drawbridge and flying carpets overhead, like fireflies in japan, with sandals and sheep and sparkling armour like joan of arc's at the very least, but there were only houses analogous to our own except prettier, less old and smaller, as if they were baby houses if what I think is a baby is correct. I spotted the church right away, as you can imagine, you don't teach an old dog new theology. I left my spade against a tree, telling myself I'd find it there on my way home, since the village didn't seem to be swarming with ferocious beasts.

And the first amazing thing that happened to me, cross my heart, was the bells, because they were ringing and I'd never made the connection. Let me explain. I said you don't teach an old dog et cetera because churches and all that, after all, I knew a thing or two about them, ever since I'd been old enough to remember being hit, father had taught us all the things in a church inside and out, using pictures in the dictionary — the nave, the rood screen, the transept, the steeple, and all the rest. Papa forced us to learn that and he was in no laughing mood, as proof I'll just mention the whacks, do you think we enjoyed them? To the question: What do bells do? I invariably replied do-o-o-ong . . . do-o-o-ong . . . , because you couldn't trip me up and that was the right answer, but I'd never made the connection with the reverberations we'd hear now and then if the wind was blowing from the pine grove towards the house, I'd always thought that the sound came to us from the clouds, that they made a kind of music by merging together or bumping into each other like well-rounded bellies, what can I say, but now I realized that it had actually been the well-known do-o-o-ong . . . do-o-o-ong . . . of church bells, and how on earth could I have guessed that? There are no bells in the steeple of the chapel on our estate and I'm no prophet. I was so moved by my discovery that without further ado I plunked myself down on the steps of the church like one man, I thought it was such a sad sound, and I sobbed a little at the sadness of the sound, because it came to us from the earth and the clouds told us nothing, they just boomed. But I didn't come here to have fun, I told myself.

And the second amazing thing, I hadn't set foot in the village for more than three minutes when I saw a neighbour and somehow or other I guessed that neighbour was a blessed virgin or a slut. The creature was dressed in black, something a number of my neighbours seem to have in common if I'm any judge, and walked hunched over, so much that it was a pity, she must have spent even more time on earth than father, for a comparison between the condition of her face and a wrinkled potato suggested itself powerfully to one's mind, that's the way it is. She looked at me with let's say astonishment, the way you look at something that's not a pleasing sight, or so it seemed, and she folded her arms to hold her purse against her inflations, which didn't strike me as vital because I had no desire for that purse and anyway she was across the street from me and horse was between us, you see.

"Papa is dead!" I shouted at her. But did she even understand the sounds I was making with my mouth? I couldn't decide what sex she was just from looking at her, whether she was a blessed virgin or a slut or et cetera, because of my lack of experience and so forth, and because dictionaries can't explain everything, because, you have to believe me, I know my limits. Nor can you trust inflations on something like this, I myself am walking proof of that. All the same, I wanted to show her my irreproachable intentions as best I could, I don't like to see suffering for no reason. I shouted at her again: "May god be with you, old slut!" Because I had one chance in two.

But I wasn't there to bless my neighbours, so once my tears had run dry I set out farther along the village road. I don't know where this audacity came from, I think I was sustained by my feeling of duty towards father. What reasons had I had before to address any neighbours when my late father was there, but now that he was no longer around to defend himself someone was going to have to take on the job, as well as find him a pine suit, and that put the wind into every one of my sails. I noticed moreover that, having disobeyed papa by stepping outside the enclosure of the estate, once that boundary had been crossed I could pass through the others as easily as I passed, in summertime, in the little woods, through the spiderwebs set with silver droplets that stayed in my hair like morning stars, so there.

General Store was written out in full in black and white. Sorry, excuse me, but the secretarious knows how to read. It was a house with big windows where you could see all kinds of goods. I left horse in the middle of the road, I went inside with my cents. There were a lot of things you see at home but in very large quantities, food for instance, in cardboard boxes, and a thing you don't ever see at home, which was a bambino, that's what it's called, it came up to about my knee. I asked it if I could trade my cents for a grave box, but I might as well have asked the pile of white pebbles the colour of father's corpse that were at the bottom of the dried-up stream. I put my hand on the bambino's skull where it was blond and soft, and that did something to me, I swear. It's because more than once in the illustrations my brother and I had seen bambinos rising up into the air like balloons because of the little wings on their backs that they keep for a certain number of years as a reminder of limbo, as long as they haven't been shed, and hang on, honey bee! — you're not pulling the ascension trick on me before I'm done with you. So as I was saying, I put my hand on its head, but maybe it couldn't comprehend the sounds that sprang from my tongue as if from an amazingly bouncy springboard, who knows? Words form within the enclosure of my cheeks and my tongue sweeps them outside with unimaginable swiftness, and perhaps it all went over the head of the bambino, which even though it had wings only came up to my thigh. And so, in an attempt to mimic mortal remains to make myself understood, I stood there all stiff with my eyes shut, I pointed to my upper lip because of papa's moustache et cetera, and then I indicated some boxes with the tip of my nose, hoping it would make the connection, but as you can imagine. And then along came a slut.

Who appeared out of the back of the shop, which is what it's called. She was wearing a black dress as you might expect, on her head was a little hat that I thought was the strangest object in the world in this country, with a grey veil that fell down over her eyes as if there were things that she didn't want to see or that she agreed to see only if they were muffled, like when you put your hand in front of a light that's too bright, and she was pulling on a glove. She told me that she was closed on account of the exceptional reason of the burial and I replied, well that's just it, thinking: News travels fast. Not seeing her eyes prevented me from determining whether she was of my calibre in the intelligence department or whether she came up no higher than kid brother's cap, which set my teeth on edge because, apart from the eyes, what is there to distinguish someone from his future mortal remains, I ask you? And there I was doing my utmost. But just try explaining to a slut that before you can bury, you need a grave box to put in the pit! She said again, I'm closed, I'm closed, you don't understand. Being closed is no reason not to do your duty, I told her and, exasperated as I had every right to be, about to explode then and there and any old way, like a shell, I nonetheless controlled myself and declared:

"It's very simple. You and your bambino give me the

coffin, I give you my cents, we put the mortal remains inside, and then we dig the pit that goes with it, on the edge of the pine grove."

And wham. Her sudden sobs bewildered me. I couldn't see how father's death could drive her to such sorrow, because papa spent almost all his time on earth with us, so nothing justified this slut's being attached to him to the point of weeping at the news of his corpse, had *I* cried? — yet I was his son, as true as I'm standing. She disappeared into the back with a handkerchief to her nose, taking the bambino with her, which was looking at me with its finger in its mouth, and I heard her say: "You deal with it, please, I can't take any more." Ah la la. I saw two men arriving, that's fate. I sighed inwardly at the thought that in this life it's absolutely pointless to try to explain yourself, I'll let you guess what colour their suits were. How strangely everyone was dressed, in fact! I can't help adding a word about this. It was as if they weren't living in their clothes. I don't know if they donned new ones every day or what, they must not be used to the sight of individuals who've lost their father, they looked at me as if I had a horn in the middle of my forehead. One of them came up to me. He took hold of my shoulders gently, in fact his gentleness did something to me, to push me towards the exit I'd come in through, and these are the very words he said:

"Try to understand, she's burying her husband."

He gave me the name of a special death shop at the other end of the street, where I could find a coffin if that was what I was looking for, but he also told me that it was closed today on account of the funeral, ditto for the town hall where I apparently had to register my own dead. He also discreetly handed me a card which I'm pasting in here, after wetting it with my long ox-tongue:

```
┌─────────────────────────────────────────┐
│                                           │
│              Rosario DUBÉ                 │
│     Lawyer, Notary, Justice of the Peace  │
│       12 Main Street, Saint-Aldor         │
│                                           │
└─────────────────────────────────────────┘
```

I met up with horse in the middle of the road and I could see in his eyes that he wanted to know if my steps had taken me where I wanted to go, and I had to admit that they hadn't. I grabbed hold of his chops and sadly led him away. We were walking along at loose ends, and a sorry sight we were, because what kind of impression would I make if I came back to my brother without a coffin after such a failure? I sat down on a front stoop very close to a dog turd, recognizable by its noble form, and I was sitting there on its account, since some flies had gathered there. For the frog which is our only toy, or just about, we have to stock up now and then in order to feed her the way I've already described, and when it comes to catching flies there's nobody like yours truly, I can even capture one in each hand simultaneously, my brother has never come close. But at this moment I had neither the morale nor the jar where we stored our dead insects for that purpose, so I simply squashed the insects inside my fist and let them fall to the ground dead, thinking, in any case, why bother?

Meanwhile the bells had stopped ringing, I don't know if I forgot to mention that, because of my hiding place I have to write too fast to reread what I've written, but I'd killed no more than nine flies when the bells started ringing again but this time there was just one, haunting and deep, like the heartbeat of a child who is going to die, if that ever happens, I mean if children die.

And then they started pouring out of houses from every

direction. If you wanted to see neighbours, this was the place! They were springing up at every turn from god knows where, I counted a hand of them, and then two hands, and then another two hands, there were at least forty-twelve of them, all more alike than the others, I thought to myself, they talk like hell but they can't scare me, then the whole group headed for the church where I had been. Horse and I were quite an odd couple or I don't know a thing, judging by their looks, which I wouldn't wish on anyone.

I got to my feet because that was the least I could do. A group formed near the general store, resembling the sheep in pictures that like nothing so much as the hole of the neighbour in front of them, for the reassuring smell, and move like one animal with fifty-thirteen hooves, which is called a myriapod. No doubt it's the custom of the country that everyone tries to resemble that day's defunct, because my neighbours all had faces as long as noodles. Have I mentioned that it was the beginning of autumn? The first dead leaves, still green, were strewn all around and I told myself that they too fit the occasion. When the red season is just beginning the disadvantage is that the flies are fewer in number, but on the other hand their flight is slower and they're easier to catch, so in a short time I'd been able to destroy two hands of them minus one finger. Be that as it may, I didn't try to join the troop. It was quite enough that they were my neighbours, I didn't have to become one of theirs even if they had permitted it, which I doubt, as you shall see. There were as many sluts and blessed virgins as the others, as far as I could judge, but not so many bambinos, clearly fewer in fact, I don't know where they could have been hidden or why, the smallest must have come up to my inflations, it was wearing an old man's hat and had a sad look on its face that made me wonder if it actually was a bambino, in any event, where wings were concerned he must have had only stumps. And the coffin came out from the general store.

A coffin — what am I saying! It was a veritable castle made of six planks. Never in my bitch of a life had I seen anything so beautiful, even horse did something he hadn't done for a moon's age, he neighed. Horse neighed! When you lavish such attention on a box, I thought, there can't be much left inside, if you want my opinion. Such concern for the container, I thought, gives the contents a hollow ring, if I'm any judge. Such an extravagant box, I thought, doesn't bode well for the emptiness inside it, believe me. A wooden fortress, I thought, to shelter nothing, and what else, and blast I can't find the words I need to say what I want to say. It happens even to me. But you ought to see what it would be like if brother were writing all this!

The slut from a while ago who was boasting that the dead man was her husband came out next, with a smug look, a handkerchief at her nose and her hand in the hand of her cherub, which appeared to be very surprised at everything around it. I felt the sympathy one orphan always feels for another, and if I'd been close enough I would have pinched it on the sly until it bled.

The crowd was transformed into a long undulating animal, a kind of snake with feet and, for the snout, a coffin I kept expecting to see a forked tongue dart out from, though according to what I've read it's rare for grave boxes to open from the inside on their own. The tail end, where I wasn't, since I was keeping my distance as you may well imagine, hadn't even started to move by the time the reptile's gleaming head penetrated the interior of the church and one of its bells began striking even in my temples, do-o-o-ong . . . do-o-o-ong . . . I stood there shifting from foot to foot, gritting my teeth with impatience, but inside my head I was telling them, faster, faster. There's one thing you have to understand though, which is that everything about a funeral has to be slow, it wouldn't be fitting to race through it, even if doing so would ultimately be in accordance with reason and the ethics of spinoza, because it would look as if you wanted to get rid of that which no longer exists, which is characterized by taking umbrage at trifles. The more one is nothing, the more one needs moral support. Whence the need to be thoughtful towards the defunct, because it's when one is dead that one needs help, whereas the living can help themselves, you can just let them croak if you want my opinion, which is exactly what happens as far as I can tell. I learned from a dictionary recently that you're supposed to put flowers on the stones above the pits where you've lowered your defunct, to prove to them beyond doubt that you didn't put them there for your amusement, that you're still thinking about them, that all things considered you'd rather they were here, and I so love the flowers no one's ever given me, like in the most wonderful stories I know, that I'd go into a pit myself if it would make my brother think of bringing me flowers while telling himself that all things considered he'd prefer to have me around, but as you can imagine. And those were my thoughts, and of course I was associating them with the still fresh memory of papa, when I saw the last of the buriers go inside the church and I stood there in the middle of the square holding horse's chops between two fingers.

WE'LL BE ACCUSED OF going inside then, horse and I, but did anyone stop to think what it was that attracted us into the holy place? It was the music. I asked myself, how could anyone dare to do that to mortal remains that are no longer there to defend themselves? I loathe music. Because music, you see, is an out-and-out debasement, a greedy octopus that feeds on us. Make music well up within a hundred-metre radius and my heart is gone, it's left my belly where it lives and burst out to the ground while I look on, bereft, even if my eyes are closed, it bounces back like an elastic and pierces a bullet hole in my chest, it's a wound that lives and is resurrected with every note and I could die a most delightful death from it, so atrocious and cruel and trying it is, just like life. To say nothing of the fact that it leaves the most horrible memories in our souls, horrible if they're good precisely because they are only memories, horrible too if the memories are horrible because it means that won't let go of us until we're on the threshold of our graves, where we don't know what lies ahead, it may be worse than what we call this side, I don't know if you follow my logic.

Be that as it may, I know whereof I speak, we had music at the house back when papa commanded everything just the day before. There were two kinds, among others. First of all there was the music that papa made himself, with his fingers and his mouth and my legs, which I'll get to in a few lines, it's worth the detour. Then there was the other kind that was produced by the fairies, but there's something I have to talk about first, which will surprise you, but believe me if you will. Papa possessed a magical generator, that's what it's called, which didn't leave his bedroom except when he carried it on his back and under his arm in the direction of the mountains past the pine grove, to fill it up, if I understood correctly, and which brother and I wouldn't touch because of the whacks. That will give you an idea of the powers father had been granted. One day he explained to us, with a jubilation that made him a very funny sight, that great forces exist in the universe, above all in the sky, for proof just look at lightning, thunder, wind, and all the rest. Now — and this is what could set dresses on fire if you don't dare believe me — you can call up those forces, which are also spirits, you can make them appear around you in eddies of flame, and if you know how to make the right movements you can capture them and put them in a box and, supposing you have the necessary ropes, you can attach that box to another box that will free the fairies imprisoned inside the black discs, which dispense the music to us, for everything in the universe communicates with everything else through the power of magic, and that's what I was getting at. Papa would wall himself up in his bedroom. We weren't allowed even to show that we were of this world by breathing, father demanded absolute silence so he could fill it with melodies, watch out for whacks. I would huddle on the other side of the door and say not a word, breathing like my friend the praying mantis. Just try to understand, in the evening mosquitoes fly to the candle that will burn them to cinders, I've often observed it, and that's me exactly in my relationship to music. Brother would snuggle up against my side, and it made him giggle, that's all he knows how to do, laugh or blubber or wriggle around on top of me. And the music would gush out with a resonance that reminded me of when my brother and I used to pinch our nostrils for the fun of it and talk through our noses. Sometimes papa's voice would rise above the melody, straddle it for a few moments, torment it just enough, and what can I tell you, it was so horribly beautiful.

But as I was saying, there was also the other kind of music

40

that papa produced with his fingers, his mouth, and my legs. You see, there was a musical instrument in the house in the midst of the dictionaries from the library, and I don't know why it wouldn't be there still in spite of everything that has shattered us over the past two days. It was an extremely complicated instrument, with three layers and a separate keyboard for each layer and pipes of different dimensions and a pump you had to activate so you could blow into the pipes, hence my legs. Brother's were stronger, I have to state things as they are, but brother would giggle as he did it and though that brought him whacks as you can well imagine he couldn't help it, as he said, so I was the one assigned by father to work the pump that blew air into the pipes, and the effort it required and the impression it made on my soul left me crying my eyes out, my head would be down and I'd push with my foot, I'd push and the tears would run down my face and, like spiders hanging from their threads, they would slide down the length of my long hair. After an hour of this regimen I was a gasping wreck, that's the name for it. All this to say nothing of the fifes, the flipple flute, and the tambourine, but those I'll discuss at the proper time, along with the billy goat and the kitten kaboodle.

And so what flabbergasted horse and me was that the music coming from the church was as close as bubbles to the music that emerged from papa's instrument with the pipes, and since, contrary to all reason, I am drawn to music that leaves me in charred shreds, we went in, horse and I, because it was inside.

And let me tell you, woe unto him by whom the offence cometh, that's the truth. I made my way up the long aisle with horse. The naked coffin was directly ahead of us. The priest was limply waving a censer, you don't teach an old dog, and his eyes were half closed and he was muttering and he looked to be thinking extremely hard about something painful, we made a conspicuous entrance, horse and I. I was holding my cents bag shoulder-high at arm's length and I showed it to the people sitting on the benches as I walked sadly, repeating, if you please, if you please, give me a coffin, and I was a pitiful sight to behold. I don't know what's happened to the hearts in this village, people don't have any, I'm telling this exactly the way it struck me. The truth compels me to say in the village's defence, however, that there was one old slut in the third row with her back all hunched over who nonetheless gave me a look without hatred, and I thought I could make out behind her grey veil that she might be aiming a smile at me that, heavens above, resembled something like compassion, just one old slut in that whole church for whom I like to think the creator of all things will reserve an easy death, like the kind experienced by flowers and butterflies, that's my wish for her, never will I forget that smile that understood. Two men grabbed me from behind and I couldn't, but. I don't know if they were the same two men as a while before at the dead man's general store, there are times when everything in the universe seems interchangeable to me, but since I was an enraged goat I had time to scream at the top of my lungs: "You're torturing your dead man with that music." I said that right to their faces, to as many of them as were there, minus the old slut with the smile, which I had time to return during that one brief moment. There were just two of them, I may have forgotten to mention that, I mean the two men who grabbed me from behind like cowards, and they were clearly stronger, we are helpless against nature's laws.

Now horse was so overwhelmed by what was happening to us that he was beside himself, he sprang out of the church and he was off like a shot, at a speed I wouldn't have thought him capable of, in the opposite direction from which we'd travelled together on the road until then, neighing, his belly level with the ground, and heading for the pine grove beyond which lay our house and papa, who still didn't have his coffin. It can't be! They left me in the middle of the road beyond the church steps, a threatening forefinger wagged at me and gave me orders but it was too late, I had reached the point of understanding absolutely nothing about anything, I was in the grip of a stoppit.

I don't know how long I stayed there in the public square, because when I have a stoppit time contracts or expands or goes in circles, it's impossible to know, it only starts bolting in a straight line once I've begun to move again, but the devil knows what happened to the hours in between. To see my hand upraised, strained, the fingernails digging into the sky, my head motionless on one side, my eyes staring at some sensationally insignificant object, to see my gaping mouth, and my buttocks raised as if a comet were about to explode from them, you might think I was a stone, but what you don't know is that when I have a stoppit I'm extremely active on the inside. I look through my ruminant eyes as I would look through a window with the eyes we have inside our bonnets, I observe everything in every direction so that nothing escapes me, I climb inside my body as if I were hiding in an attic and spying on the world through the bull's eye, ah la la, another eye. If I move my little finger, the one you use to scratch your hole, the cosmos is liable to fly into smithereens, that will give you an idea of how I feel when I have a stoppit. Sometimes I can't do a thing, one leg starts to tremble and oh it's terrible the anguish it creates, it's as if the earth is rumbling and I have to control my leg without using my hands if I'm to prevent universal disaster, and it takes much more effort than pumping a pipe organ, that's what it's called. Papa was also subject to stoppits, I don't know if I forgot to mention that. It runs in the family.

The fact remains that the moment came when they all streamed out of the church behind the coffin, it made you wonder if they were going to follow it into the grave and be buried with it out of some idiotic fascination, like our former dog that wouldn't let go of me at those times when I was dripping disgusting blood. In fact that was why father finally put mothballs in his daily bread. Later on I'll explain about all that blood business, which must seem strange, and is, as a matter of fact.

And so the crowd in the street. Apparently they hadn't yet got used to having me as a neighbour, judging by their expressions, which I wouldn't wish on anyone. The whole lot of them started forming a circle around me and it was terrible, that's all I can say, and I was beginning to panic in my attic, so much that it pulled me out of my stoppit a little. I began to swivel on my left leg by fits and starts, like the beggar on his fool's bauble, being careful not to change the position of the other parts of my body, I don't know if I'm making myself understood, and as the circle around me came undone, people shrank back as if they were afraid of getting involved in something about me that was none of their business. How long I stood like that, turning clockwise, I don't know but, freed even slightly from my stoppit, I regained the notion of time, and it seems to me that I kept swivelling like that as long as the rank of the faithful hadn't been stitched back together and people hadn't finished disappearing at the end of the street to go and bury their dead, or so I assume, it makes no difference to me. But they didn't all follow, for a reason I'd very much like to have explained to me because I don't know what it is, and a few remained and observed me as if I were the pope's shit, I mean with intense curiosity, and moved away a few paces and then came to a standstill once more to stare at me, then moved away again, and they kept this up till I couldn't see anyone anywhere and there I was alone and sadly forsaken on the village square, as if I were the surviving prince in a kingdom devastated by cholera. An impressive silence underscored by the sound of leaves tumbling in the wind, if you want my opinion.

And finally, because such things happen on this earth, there were two individuals before me, two again, it's as if they go around in pairs, these sly devils whose outfits I give up trying to describe, aside from the one on my right, who was wearing a soutane and wasn't the priest I'd seen before but was much younger, waving the censer around the dead man.

"Who are you?" asked the other one.

Fearing whacks, I pretended I hadn't heard.

"Where are you from?" added the soutane. "From the house on the other side of the pine grove? What are you doing here?"

As you may imagine, I didn't dare mention the coffin for fear it would lead to more marmalade stews for me because I was getting to know a thing or two in that department. Don't speak of rope in the house of a hanged man.

"Follow us," said the soutane, putting his hand gently on my shoulder, in fact his gentleness did something to me.

He added: "We won't hurt you," which was something at least. My stoppit now just a memory among others, I followed them. As long as you don't hurt me, you see, you can get anything from me, that's the lesson to be drawn. It's because I was born under the astronomical sign of the ass that I'm like this, in the manner of calves and piglets.

I FOLLOWED THEM, and I tried to be a pitiful sight with my mouth and my eyes and all my airs and graces so they'd treat me nicely, so they would help my heart in all this suffering, so they'd think I was a handsome youth. The priest didn't look nasty. Because his soutane was all dungy and covered with chalk dust I felt safe, he looked more like a neighbour than the others, papa had been a priest too when he was a fine-looking lad. The other individual had a revolver in his belt, which startled me, because from the pictures I'd seen I had always thought firearms were very small, whereas in reality, my goodness, this one was as big as father's balls.

While I walked I rememoried in bits and pieces what our life had consisted of to date, and what it would no longer be as everything passes here below, for instance the sound that papa made upstairs while he was doing his exercises, or when we all ate together and we tied a bib around our frog for a laugh and fed her flies, and the care that papa lavished on the Fair Punishment in the woodshed when he took it out of its box, which would now be more berefted than ever, I thought about all that and it helped me be a pitiful sight because it turned me every which way in my sadness and I felt something like an urge to cry. It's a pretty word, rememory, I don't know if it actually exists but it means to recall things.

Now I'd like you to pay close attention because what comes next will be difficult.

First of all they showed me into the town hall, that's what it's called according to what I could read above the door, and it was a very pretty house, so clean that you felt like applauding and walking around inside dressed like adam and dancing barefoot among the manikins of light. We walked down a corridor, which evoked for me the portrait gallery on our estate, I'll certainly have something to say about that

46

later because of the sudden light these portraits would shed, a few hours from now, on my own origins here below, then we entered a small room equipped with tables, seats, and lamps that were attached to the wall by ropes and created light through the power of magic. The two men who accompanied me hadn't said a word to me along the way but between themselves they talked a great deal, energetically and anxiously it seemed to me, and the priest said officer to the man who was wearing the firearm with its breathtaking dimensions. The first thing I noticed in this little room was that there was someone else inside it, at first I could see only the feet crossed on a desk and the hands because a screen concealed the head, but right away I felt safe because the hands were opening a dictionary entitled the flowers of evil. They sat me down and then the officer's questions began.

"You live in the house on the other side of the pine grove, don't you? And your father is mister soissons? And it's his horse that was with you?"

I moved my torso from side to side as if I were humming a little song inside my bonnet, I stared vacantly into space, but I didn't reply. Incidentally, the strange thing about that word soissons is that sometimes I would nod off in the middle of my dictionaries and all at once, perfectly clearly, I would hear the word soissons whistle very quickly past my ear and flee like a trout that slips between our legs when we walk barefoot in the lake in summer, and I had the impression that the word had something to do with me, that it belonged to the most intimate part of me more than any other word, I'm saying it the way it seems to me, and that word soissons brought me out of my dozing all surprised.

The priest and the officer went on reviling me with questions, and it seemed that I annoyed them with the way I appeared not to hear the vulgate, but I meant no harm and they got lost in conjecture and other calculations of the sort and, let me tell you, even though I had the strongest sense of such things, never would I have believed that my father was such an important man. The officer even had a big grey moustache as if he wanted to imitate him! That moustache was so much like his, you'd have thought it had flown from papa's face like my friend the dragonfly, as it's said that our soul flies away when we die, and had settled above the lip of the officer, as true as I'm.

The gentleman in question, along with the soutane, soon opted for speaking to me as if they'd known me all my life, thinking that would sound better between my ears, and when they asked me if something had happened to my father I finally showed them that I understood the human tongue like everybody else, and I answered, he died this morning at dawn, which made an impression.

They asked me to repeat it, it was a piece of news that would travel far if proved correct, but repeating isn't my strong point. "We found him hanging this morning at the end of a rope that he was clinging to like one man without a by-your-leave," I said instead. The priest made the sign of the cross on his belly. The officer seemed calmer. Mind you, he didn't have a crucifix around his neck that he'd be constantly tempted to play with, the way kid brother does with you know what. He told me in a voice full of tact, as if I were something infinitely fragile that had to be treated sensitively:

"You said, 'We found him.' Who is we?"

"Papa has two sons," I said. "Me and my brother."

They drew back their necks in stupefaction the way pigeons do when they walk, they gazed at me as if I'd said something outrageous, just try to understand them, my contemporaries and friends. The officer moved his hand as if to say, we'll come back to that later, and he asked me:

48

"What about your mama? Isn't there a mother living with you?"

"There have never been any sluts in our house," I said.

From the look on their faces I realized clarifications were called for, so I added:

"All mothers are sluts but you can say blessed virgins too if you fancy, the nuance is infinitesimal."

I received two very quick whacks from the man in the soutane, one with the flat of the hand, the other with the back, both with the right hand and in less time than it takes to write it down. I'd have liked to put my fingers in my underwear and flick blood at him, but I didn't have any blood that day, it had healed over until next time.

Then the third man, of whom I'd so far seen only the hands and feet, got out of his chair and I immediately recognized my neighbour who'd come to my house to importune me, the prince that brother teased me about and said I was in love with, humph. He seemed interested in everything we were saying but he said nothing himself, in the manner of cats and wise men. He had crossed his arms and he rested his shoulder against the wall and he was looking at me with curiosity and gravity for some reason I'm unaware of, maybe he was in love too. Just seeing him gave me a kind of urge to run my tongue all over his face, to put his nose in my mouth, things sometimes happen in my head and in my body that are genuine riddles for me. He still had his dictionary in his hand and he'd made a bookmark with one of his fingers and I liked that detail because it was something I very often did too when I broke off my reading to dream about the handsome knights the pages talked about, I'd make a bookmark with one of my fingers. As for the priest, he had withdrawn to a chair in the corner and he was staring at the floor with eyes like saucers. For a man who had promised not to harm me, it struck me that, despite the soutane he was wearing, his word had no more weight than a comet that emerges from our hole.

But getting back to sluts, I tried to explain to them that I did indeed have a very distant rememory of a blessed virgin who'd held me on her knees and smelled good, and even of a cherub on the sweet-smelling virgin's other knee who was as much like me as a bubble, as my brother tried to convince me. But was that a memory? And was she a slut?

The priest had come back and with a stunned look, like the one kid brother had the time he told me dog had just died, whereas I didn't give a hoot owl as my father would say, he repeated: "She's crazy. Or possessed." Soutanes don't know the genders of pronouns, if I'm any judge. What's more, I don't know what that priest did with his saliva but in the corners of his lips he had a sort of dry verdigris foam, mouth-kelp if you'll believe me, that I was seeing for the first time on a neighbour, I don't know if it's rare or what, in any case I have a horror of it, if you'll give credence to these words of mine. For want of blood I flicked contempt at him with my eyes, which were always filled with little thunderbolts according to my late father.

They started talking between themselves again, I mean the officer and the priest, with no concern for me aside from the glances they shot at me now and then, glances that froze them for a moment in a kind of horrified stupor, and I'm choosing my words carefully. But there was also the prince and he was observing me with touchingly friendly eyes and when I saw him smile at me I turned my face away, shrugging and putting on airs, because who did he think I was anyway?

The serious matter that seemed to overwhelm the other two, which they kept harping on like a refrain, was the fact that my late father was the owner of the mine and his death was going to cause changes, and they seemed to have a horror of change if you want my opinion. They finally told me that I was going to be obliged to take them to papa.

"Papa has disappeared."

"What's that? What do you mean? Have you lost his remains?"

"His body is there," I said, "but he himself has disappeared."

That shouldn't be hard to understand.

"Then you'll have to take us to his remains."

To show them that such a thing was completely out of the question I went into a stoppit. Don't worry, it wasn't a real one, it was just to impress them, which it did. The prince said gently, his gentleness even et cetera:

"Can't you see you're frightening her? She's trembling."

Another one who thought I was a slut, I suppose he was going by my inflations and I told him so with my eyes.

"Mister mine inspector, I would ask you not to get mixed up in this. Go back to your poems." It was the officer who said that to the prince.

"Precisely. As mine inspector it seems to me that it does concern me just a little, don't you think?"

Those two seemed not to like each other, to put it in black and white. I must also point out that the officer had in common with my brother the fact that he looked like someone who never sticks his nose in a dictionary, which fills such people with jealous contempt for those who make a bookmark with a finger, and I thought to myself that even though he'd called me a slut, in the event of out-and-out warfare I wouldn't make a big fuss, I would side with the mine inspector, all daggers drawn. What can you do with someone who never sticks his nose in a dictionary?

The priest and the mustachioed officer concluded that it was a case of force majeure and that it was their duty to advise the mare, who had been prevented from following the grocer's funeral by the flu, and I told myself that they definitely knew nothing about what words mean, but then I realized that no doubt they meant mayor and not mare, because watch out! — the secretarious is a reader. They told the mine inspector to keep an eye on me in the meantime and then they were off like gushes of piss.

I'll tell you, had I been able to foresee that I'd be having a tête-à-tête with the mine inspector before the day was over, I think, all things considered, I'd rather have hanged myself with papa's rope, because I was a little frightened by the urges of my heart, to say the least, and according to the dictates of nature and religion it's obviously my brother I should fittingly be in love with, not another man.

THE FIRST THING THE PRINCE did once we were alone and given over to his mercy was ask me if I wanted a coffee or a cup of milk or a glass of cider or god knows what, I only admitted that I was as thirsty as a sponge in the sun, those were my very words.

"How old would you be? Sixteen? Seventeen?"

Then, since I'd rather have let myself be chopped up fine than answer him, he added with a taunting little laugh:

"You're the same age as your heart, I suppose?"

I couldn't help myself: "At the age of my heart I'd be ninety or more."

"Do you know what you've just done?" he asked as he put some water on to heat. "Without knowing it you've just made an anapestic tetrameter."

I've spent my life amid crud and mud and let me tell you, I had no idea what you measured with a tetrameter. But I'm just reporting what was said to me, I'm not trying to understand. To tell the truth, I don't know exactly how long I've been on this earth, but it seems to me that it's been a long time. I have more memories than if I were a thousand. To heat the water, the mine inspector had gone to the other side of his desk, I'm not sure I remembered to tell you that, and as he was speaking quite quietly and abstractedly I couldn't always hear exactly what he said, but it didn't seem to be very important either to him or to me. For me his voice was enough. I mean that it was like music, and it turned me inside out the same way, causing me exquisite suffering, I had an urge to lie on the ground on my belly and have him stretch out motionless on my back and go on talking to me.

I say abstractedly because, while he was fussing with the cups and the coffee, he kept darting a worried and reflective glance at an open notebook. I saw him pick up a pencil and correct a word or I'll eat my boots.

"Are you a secretarious?" I asked.

He asked me to say it again. But too bad for him, I need words too much to waste them by saying them twice. I kept silent. Then he gave a little sigh tinged with a shade of disdain, similar to the one that I give when, flushed with emotion, I gaze at my reflection in water just dipped from the well in the spring, because of the colour of my eyes, and my brother catches me and makes fun of me and I tell him, feigning indifference: "How tiresome these mirrors are, how tiresome! . . ." That's why I didn't believe in the inspector's indifference when he let drop, after his sigh:

"Let's say that I try to write poems . . ."

Poems, all right, I know what they are, there are lots of them in my dictionaries of chivalry. I was joking a while ago when I made believe that I thought a tetrameter was something to measure with. You don't understand a thing about yours truly unless you understand his sense of humour.

"I write too," said I, sighing likewise.

He stared at me in a way that made my inflations feel all warm, and my thighs too, because the power of magic connects those parts. If my brother looked at me like that more often, I thought to myself, life would be an enchanted forest. That put words in my mouth:

"You see, father made each of us in turn assume the role of secretarious. The onus of such a task falls to the sons, that's what he told us in his stentorian voice (I don't know what a stentorian is). Even though I did it willingly, without looking pitiful, and my brother's stomach heaved at the mere thought of it, brother was required to put in his days with the book of spells too, days interspersed with mine, and just reading what we'd written would make us laugh if we were in a laughing mood because there are times, and I'm saying this in black and white, when all brother does is pretend, doodling lines with his pencil, my brother is an idiot, a real ninnycompoop. Despite the fact that when father checked in the book of spells it broke my heart, because he couldn't tell the difference, humph. That didn't keep me from being the more intelligent of his sons. But with father dead, people will have to walk over my body before they take away my book of spells, and as for brother, he doesn't give a damn, he won't look pitiful, he'll go on living a life of dissipation."

The inspector had approached me with the coffees and I think I can say from the way he was behaving that he thought I was someone who deserved to live. He hesitated before a fair number of his sentences, his lips moved but the words didn't come out. Finally he said:

"Why do you always talk about yourself as if you were a boy? And your accent, where on earth did you get that . . . Don't you know you're a girl? And even, I'd say," — his lips uncovered all his teeth, which made me think of the sunshine when it clears a little path for itself between two clouds on our estate — "and even, I would say, a very *very* pretty one."

And I swear, he said that second *very* in italics.

"Maybe a little grimy," he added, because nothing is unalloyed beneath the salt of heaven, not even kind words, and he took out his handkerchief and wiped my cheek with it, but I jerked my head back. I tell you, I abhor that handkerchief and I would love to have it in my hand right now, I think I'd squeeze it very hard between my legs, but since he still thought I was a slut I felt obliged to explain, it's my own personal cross that I'm always having to explain myself in great detail to those I love, as horse is my witness:

"And does mister priest who hit me also have inflations under his dress? Once upon a long time ago a true calamity happened to me, I think I lost my balls. I bled for days and then it healed over and then it started up again, it depends on the moon, ah la la, it's all because of the moon, and I started to get inflations on my torso as well. My brother laughed because my father made me wear this skirt so the blood wouldn't overflow and leave a stain, and I got angry when my brother laughed and I'd chase after him so I could flick fingers full of blood at his face. Even when I was little, what I remember is that father and brother pissed standing up but I always crouched down, because I never wanted to touch my balls or even just look at them the way my brother does all the time, I didn't actually feel them till the day I lost them, if that makes any sense, and then I started bleeding. But it makes no difference, father knew I was the more intelligent of his sons, and shoo. Balls or no balls."

He didn't seem to find what I told him very clear but I can't help that, when I say things I always say them the way they are and if they seem strange it's not the fault of my bonnet, blame the things themselves. He sat facing me and stared at me very impolitely, and sometimes with an amused smile, as if I were a little show starring just me, like our only toy, our frog.

And then he started asking me questions too. But he did it with the intention of helping me, I was well aware of that, and it made me feel better when I answered him. Since he wanted to know why I'd come to the village, I replied that I'd come for a grave box, also called a coffin in the vulgate, and that I was most aggrieved at not having found one, and in so saying I put on an air that was quite pitiful, I think. He asked what my brother was like and I replied that he was an idiot who was always laughing and crying and who pulled my hair when I was reading the memoirs of the duc de saint-simon or made me smell the oozing from his sausage on his fingertips, but the purpose of his question was to know if he was younger or older than me, which I eventually understood. I declared that papa had kneaded us on the same day at exactly the same hour, a good long while ago apparently, according to religion.

Using his thumb and his index finger the mine inspector rubbed his eyelids as if he had a pain in his noggin. Then he stretched his legs out under the table and began to reflect during a long minute of silence, hands crossed behind the back of his head, as true as I'm. His eyes were like those of an owl, vast, with light standing inside them. Then he leaned towards me and said, with the little voice you use in certain dreams when you're talking to something that doesn't exist:

"Do you know that your father was rich? Fabulously rich?"

With my nose, I pointed to my cents bag. I let him draw his own conclusions. The truth is that for some time I'd been feeling a need to be outside. It's hard for me to be inside a house for a long time, even in my own or in the woodshed with the Fair Punishment, which will astonish people, and to get to sleep at night I sometimes lie down in the landscape with my face all wet from the field stars. That sensation comes back to my memory because I'm in the woodshed now as I write this and I'm starting not to be able to hold on, I feel as if I'm going to start screaming but I mustn't.

The inspector told me that I was no doubt also unaware that what he called my family was a genuine mystery to my neighbours in the village. Apparently no one knew exactly what transpired on our side of the pine grove, and people told all sorts of tales, ah la la, those filthy gossips. Furthermore, he thought he was teaching me that father was the most powerful man in the region, as if I could be ignorant of such a thing, and that was why, he went on, no one would ever have dared go against his orders. Without a formal invitation, no one had the right to venture into our estate, you see! Not even the priest.

"I know something about that, the mayor preached to me about it for an hour when I came to see you last spring, when I first arrived in this part of the country. Do you remember me? I talked to you . . . Incidentally, what's your name?"

"Brother calls me brother, and father called us son when he commanded everything just the day before."

"And how did you know which one of you he was speaking to?"

"Most of the time, one or the other, it made no difference to him. But if we really did make a mistake, if I reported when he called and brother was the one he wanted, he would simply say: 'Not you, the other one.' It never caused anyone any problems."

"I see."

He saw! The gentleman saw! Who did he think he was anyway? swear, some people are like that, as my father liked to say when he talked about the days when he was a fine-looking lad. But the gentleman in question, the secretarious of poems, didn't stop at that, as you may well imagine, and the limits were overstepped when that brazen and ill-mannered fellow declared:

"Would you like me to give you a name that's just for me? Wild one. I'll call you wild one. It goes well with your perfume of grass and rain. Mine is paul-marie. If you like."

I'll tell you, wild one has a fringe of hair on his forehead, it's the only place papa cut my hair, around the beginning of every season he would take out the kitchen knife and slice, but the rest of it is very long and very black and very luxuriant and very fragrant, it's true, and as he smiled at me with urges standing in his eyes like candles, the mine inspector took a lock of my hair that was tickling my cheek and gently tucked it behind my ear. I didn't hesitate for one moment, I put it back in the very same place on my cheek, where it was perfectly fine, thank you very much. That made him laugh. He brought his face closer to mine. And then, what can I say, it happened by itself, I have no other explanation, I gave him a long lick on his cheek with my tongue, which surprised him so much that he shrank back into his chair.

He wiped his cheek with the back of his hand, not briskly and energetically as if he were disgusted but with a sort of surprised affection, the way papa used to stroke my brother's hair after he'd let loose a storm of whacks that had left him on the floor amid the pumpkins. I have no idea what kind of look I gave the mine inspector then, but it must have been worth its weight in little thunderbolts, I don't know if I'm making myself understood.

"I see . . ." (He was seeing again!) "You're a wild little goat, is that it?"

He said this with a sardonic smile, if sardonic means what I think it means, but I could see his green pallor and the intense fear in his beautiful blue eyes, because I don't know if I remembered to say this but, as for the inspector, the wild little goat thinks he has the eyes of a knight with his great brackmard sword, which is what we say about a sophisticated suit of armour, if my memory's not playing tricks.

In any event I can't explain what happened next, really, how he suddenly found himself standing right up against me, disasters happen here below, and better things, things we'll never understand no matter what, but my teeth nibbled at his cheek and I licked his nose, his forehead, his eyelids, his hair overflowing my hands. I felt his palms running all over me, as if he wanted to hold every part of me at the same time, he pressed me as if he wanted to thrust me into the interior of his person, which was fragrant with the odours of cedar, celery, and fir, while I, I died every time and I wanted to die again and I wanted it to begin again at every moment and forever, but soon it was beyond the strength of the little goat, who stood there limp, dead, arms dangling, mouth brimming with the salty taste of a knight's skin on his tongue.

Then why did he suddenly grab hold of my wrists? He stepped back, there was a look of dread on his face. "We mustn't!" he said and it was a horrified whisper, I'm choosing my words carefully. I freed my wrists from his embrace, I didn't have all my faculties, they were wandering on their own I know not where, the little goat lay down on his slightly bulging belly at the feet of the knight and I wished he would stretch out on top of me with all his weight, with all his length, with all the dignity of his person while he spoke close to my ear and didn't move, but he threw himself so to speak to the other end of the room, you'd have thought he was trying to run away, and it was, how can I put it? It was precisely as if someone had planted a dagger right in my heart, or my name's not wild one.

AND SINCE I'M A SHY LITTLE GOAT, a spurned one, a failed one even, because a certain individual doesn't want to take the trouble to make my existence happy for a few moments, his entire person stretched out full length on my back, I'm going to use the gender of sluts for my pronouns now, though I'm still my father's son and my brother's brother as religion would say. I mean that, as I relate the rest of my sorrows and lamentations, I'll speak about myself as if I were a blessed virgin with inflations and seasonal streams of blood, that will relieve the tedium of my distress, but here I must pause to explain something: the shed where I'm writing, also known as the vault.

I've taken refuge in the shed where I'm writing because my brother has been touched by grace and it has driven him mad, that's what you call it, and I panicked. I'm frightened too because there's a basement window with amazingly dirty panes in the vault where I'm writing and I was able to clean one small corner of it by rubbing with my little fist, which allowed me to notice someone coming along the road just now, and I still don't know who it is because he's so far away but maybe it's a horse and maybe it's a knight or maybe it's just the beggar hopping on his fool's bauble like a magpie. I've felt urges to start screaming, strewth, but I mustn't. Now that I've provided this clarification, which frees my chest where I was beginning to suffocate, let's go back to my romance with the mine inspector at the town hall, because you have to call a spade a spade, after all.

The inspector came back to me while I was still lying there in all the dignity of my full length, and told me not to lie there like a stalk of boiled asparagus but to get up, he spoke in a voice filled with pity and sweetness but I'll tell you, just then pity was very far from what I was feeling. I reflected for a moment, while I looked at his thrilling shoes the size of firearms, as to whether it was worth the trouble to start living again after such an assault of disdainment. I don't know if that word exists but it deserves to. I finally got back on my feet and that was too bad. If we had to come up with reasons to go on breathing, the earth would be as naked as an egg. I have fingernails as hard and sharp as tacks, I planted one of them under the eye of my handsome knight and pulled down, true as I'm. He grabbed my wrist and this time he squeezed very hard as if to hurt me too, like the priest. On the back of his neck I saw red patches of great emotion which reminded me of the ones father and brother displayed once a year, when we all laughed together and we could barely stand on our feet from drinking fine wine, it was to celebrate the friday when jesus died. The inspector had three fine lines of blood, daughters of my own hand, like beads on his cheek. He stared at me, breathing very hard, I could see he was scared fitless.

"You're a genuine witch . . ."

I hurled my head sharply against his, like a cannon shot really, my tongue all the way out to lick the blood on his face, which I desperately wanted to do. He threw back his chest. Then he forced me, brutally is the word, to sit back down in my chair. I couldn't resist but I knitted my brow and gritted my teeth. He wanted to impress me too, because he started talking very fast. He didn't dare look me in the eye though, and I could see that I had triumphed, boiled asparagus or not.

I didn't know what lay ahead for me, poor little girl, he said. Everything was going to be different now for brother and me. There would be all sorts of problems with the inheritance but that, he imagined, was three hundred feet over my head, wasn't it? (I nodded.) One thing was certain, father wouldn't be there to protect us, he went on. The law would take charge of the matter et cetera and we, my brother and I, would be at the mercy of all those people.

I don't know whom he meant by all those people but he pointed with his thumb as if they were invisible somewhere in the room. I also don't know what he meant by the law, which he was making such a fuss about, or what. Then the inspector delivered the final blow by saying, in a way that could drill a hole in your chest just like that:

"I doubt if your brother and you will be able to go on living on your estate."

In a flash I was out of the room. I ran, groping my way, holding my stomach as if it were about to overflow, and on the way to exit of the building, that's what you call it, the mine inspector caught up with me.

"I'll try to help you, I promise," he said, trying to catch his breath. "I don't yet know how but I'll try. I'll do my best to buy you time till tomorrow, I'll tell them I made you promise to come back with your brother, I'll do everything I can to rebuild your house . . ."

I don't know what he said after that because I had disappeared. I ran full tilt through the village all the way to the edge of the road that goes through the pine grove, where I found horse waiting for me. I pitched, yes that's the word, I pitched the cents bag into the thicket and flung three gobs of spit after it to ward off evil spells. I rubbed my scalp frantically with my fists, as if I wanted to make little demons fall from it. At last I got my breath back and I was a little calmer. With his teeth horse had picked up the spade that I'd left against a tree when I'd come here, he was looking at me with his worried gaze, I told him everything. I could see that he was suffering too, that there was crying in his round eyes. I told him to go on ahead of me so he'd arrive at our estate sooner and reassure brother, who must have been fretting to death when he saw the day vanish without us.

All this had left me worn out and distraught, and I was moving along with the sensation that everything in my head was going to crumble into an avalanche of ashes. And I felt exhausted and sick to my stomach, as if everything about my health was askew. I stopped to snap off some twigs and stick them into my long hair, and I curved them to make myself a crown of thorns, then I walked in such a way that you would have said I was dancing despite my sorrow. My hands are full of grace, I don't know if I forgot to say that, like the ovember waves on the pond, because I know the names of the months too, all my friends are words. I'm always surprised to note that once the first gust has passed I can be so indifferent to what might happen to me here below, it's my nature. Slowly I turn myself around with my skirt the friend of saturn who is my planet and I laugh without its showing inside the little altar of my silence, just like her. My feet move lightly, following the example of the birds that take their flight around my body, that are the colour of my eyes, for all birds waltz with me, that's my secret, even those at the other end of the earth. I've often dreamed of being able to dance on the summits of pine trees the way elves do, as warm and light as candle flames, sheaves of powdered gold would tumble from my hands to spangle the countryside with stars, I was born for that, but I can't. And then, I tell you, I would have wanted never to come back, never to return, to stay forever on the road through the pine grove, between estate and village, to be the unobtrusive divinity of the distance that separates all things, the little fairy of the paths that lead nowhere. But I plucked up my courage in both legs and continued on my way. And in doing so I found the strength to resist the great temptation I often feel to thrust things very deep between my thighs, onto my skin, sometimes even to push them inside, grass for instance, or flower buds, or pebbles as round and soft as horse's gaze. Other times I take my inflations in my hands and squeeze them till it hurts, because someone has to look after them while my mind is elsewhere, roaming in a country of my dreams, where everything pleases my heart, and where I have the misery of not existing. Bad luck can come to anyone at all, what can I say, it's a law of the universe.

All that to say that at nightfall, when I set foot in our kitchen again, I was most surprised, given the state of mind I was in, to find my brother holding a saw and getting ready to cut papa's mortal remains into pieces.

II

THERE IS A THING THAT EXISTS everywhere in the universe, according to what I've read, and that thing is communicating vessels, and how true it is. For sometimes papa would have a heavy hand with his whacks and my brother would take the rap like splinters of green wood, and afterwards I'd be subjected to my brother and that's called communicating vessels. My brother is a little bit smaller than I am but I don't know, it's as if he were made of hard rubber. When he lashes out at me there's nothing I can do but hunch my shoulders around my head and pray that the time will pass as quickly as possible. My father hardly ever had a go at me towards the end of his time on earth, in the interests of truth I even have to say that the last time goes back to a day of yore if not longer. Since then, he used only little whacks with me, when he was impatient or strictly for form, as if he didn't want to lose his touch, and to remind me that I was his son, and in the interests of truth I also have to say that the whacks he intended for me paled in comparison with those he dealt out to brother, which brother was well aware of as he snickered in his corner with sinister bitterness, for my brother is envious by nature, it's his worst flaw I think. I must say that papa considered me the more intelligent of his sons, as I think I've already written, and that I was well behaved when I had my nose in my dictionaries or when I was picking flowers and very softly singing the music of the fairies, the wild roses are pretty in the mud near the pumpkins, I wasn't always playing with my balls like you know who. And finally there was the fact that I didn't hit anyone, I'm not in the habit of doing that unless the little goat is seething with an almighty rage as you may have the goodness to recall, o my beloved who was lacerated by my nails. All this to say that it was only right if kid brother found himself, more often than he deserves, stretched out as if dead in the backyard of the house among the potatoes in their hunting jackets.

And also to say that when I saw what kind of hell he was heading for with his handsaw I wasn't worried, not in the least, and I tried as gently as a woman to quiet him down and seduce him into explaining to me, before he did it, why he seemed so intent on cutting papa into different pieces. And do you know what his reply was? His reply was:

"We have to reduce papa to ashes before we bury him."

Horse is like me and doesn't have balls, in case I've forgotten to mention that, but he still had the cord I'd wrapped around his belly like a girth so he could haul the wretched grave box, and the end of it was still hanging between his legs like a prick. For horse had entered the house behind me, an unprecedented act showing that something was beginning to go rotten in the state of denmark. He was lying on his side and the half of his big belly that lay flattened on the floor increased the volume of the other half, I think that's what I mean to say, and it reminded me of papa's chest during that sweet time when he was still breathing. The sudden and entirely unaccustomed soundness of my brother's reasoning left me flabbergasted, strewth.

"You went to the village for a coffin. Where's your coffin?"

"First of all it's not my coffin, it's papa's. And second of all I couldn't find one."

Brother snickered as I'd never heard him snicker before, though there had never been a lack of opportunities to hear him do so. He broke off sharply and shot me a very dark look, with his eyelids creased and his pupils filled with things that had been stepped on.

"We don't have a box big enough to put papa in," he said, "and it's your fault."

I gave him a scandalized look.

"Yes, your fault! So we'll burn him. We'll take his ashes, if you see what I mean, and we'll put them in his hot pepper jar so we can bury it with him inside. Now then, have you noticed the size of our oven? Try putting the mortal remains of a dead man in there! . . . We'd have to proceed by inches."

And already the teeth of the handsaw were settled on papa's leg. Listen, I've panicked at less.

"No, stop! We can't do that!"

"Have you got another solution, maybe?"

And the handsaw he was waving near my face rippled and produced a music that would have made me giggle on other days, in other ways.

"And then we're going to take all his papers and the fairies' box of magical effects and we're going to bury them along with him. And the Fair Punishment too, I'll have you know. We're going to cast all of that, and the Fair Punishment too, into the same hole!"

"The Fair Punishment?" He couldn't do that. He couldn't do that. "But we'll lose the power of speech!"

Luckily papa's mortal remains had become like stone, this morning's rigidity was spruce beer in comparison, and I knew that deep down my brother was lazy and would quickly grow discouraged in the face of such a task. Only a few sickly drops of blood had started dribbling, their colour already peculiar, the blood was thick and wouldn't move very quickly and that gave me some time to have an illumination, if it warrants that name, and eventually I did.

"They'll come to our property in gangs! Entire hordes of

neighbours! They'll take everything away from us and we won't be able to live in the kitchen any more."

That paralyzed him on the spot. "What are you saying?"

There are circumstances beyond our control when we have to repeat what we've just said, I apologize to the words. I repeated the above paragraph more or less verbatim.

Kid brother had gone green around the gills.

"I'll explain," I said, and took advantage of his stupor to remove the handsaw from his grip. Without a word he let himself be guided, his jaw gaping, and he took stunned, docile little steps, comparable to papa's after he'd knocked his skull repeatedly against a tree trunk by way of exercise. I dragged kid brother into the library.

On the matter of dictionaries, I'm sure we have more than there are trees in the pine grove, maybe even more than there are thorns on the branches of all the trees in the pine grove, myriads of them if such things exist. I don't know if I've read half of them, yet I want you to know I have read. I keep telling myself that one day I'll have devoured all of them, at least those that aren't rotten and decomposing in my hands like a damp block of flour, but I can't help myself, I always come back to my favourites, the ones that talk about magnificent cavaliers with outfits that sparkle like spoons, and the ethics of spinoza, which is baffling like all great truths, to say nothing of the memoirs of the duc de saint-simon. I don't know where in the universe all those stories took place, in what foreign lands, I find it hard to believe such things could have happened on this earth from what I've been able to see of it, especially now that I've been able to verify with my own eyes what the village looks like, which seemed to me not much compared to my imaginings, but I go into a waltz when I read the duc de saint-simon. There is dancing in the darkest shadows deep in my head, like the roar of phantom armies that vanish into smoke, for the little goat can't grasp more than a few simonian crumbs, but my chest goes up to the sky forthwith when I read him, and shoo. For instance, to avoid disputes and difficulties the king did away with all ceremonies resolving that no formal betrothals would be held in his chambers but the marriages would be performed at once taking place in the chapel to make unnecessary the wearing of the long tailed coat with flaring panels which would no longer be worn ceremoniously except by the bodyguards on duty to the princess as they wore it every day, and further that the pall would be held by the bishop of metz who had been appointed first almoner to the king as a relic of his uncle and by the district almoner of the king who would be the abbé morel by day that msgr the duc de bourgogne alone would give his hand to the princess both going to and returning from the chapel and no prince would sign the curé's book after monsieur le prince, that is a sentence from saint-simon, and if I've learned anything at all as secretarious I owe it to the duc, to his thunderous language and his extraordinary stories, to his sentence which shoots up to its summit like farts from a burning log, I beg you to believe me, if you see what I mean.

The rain that is welling up from the ground and will never end has already done its work on part of the dictionaries, a long and slow and inexorable work of invasion by mildew and damp is exerting its powers on our estate and the dictionaries are dying a natural death like all the rest — corruption! do your duty. You have to clear a path through the piles of books, that's what their actual name is, that stand higher than my brother's head and mine, and since we haven't known the wondrous lands of the cavaliers and jesus, walking amid mounds of dictionaries like that is the most intoxicating thing I've experienced on this planet up till now, with the exception of the tiny moment when we shared our transports and you deigned to hold me against your chest and my tongue ran over your face, o my valiant cavalier, or else the times when I dance with my manikins of light, as you shall see.

It was out of the question for horse to follow us, there are limits after all. I forbade it with one glance and he stayed on the threshold, a pitiful sight with his walleyes. Horse lacks only the power of speech, and even that depends on what you call speech. Brother and I sat down on some antique pillows covered with old velvet curtains that apparently, in the glorious days before our time on earth, adorned the tall windows in the library with the broken panes that let in winds and hail and swarms of snowflakes, and those antique pillows and that old velvet curtain were my bed at the times when I didn't sleep under the stars, as I recall having already written. I began explaining to brother what had taken place in the village, see above, omitting however certain details that were liable to offend my own sense of propriety, and the questions he asked me were so strange and dwelled on so many details, details so insignificant that at times I got lost myself, and it took as long as thirty-twelve days of rain but eventually he grasped the essentials, which I had him repeat like a lesson to be quite certain he'd understood the nature of the jam we were in. And after that he didn't say even a tickle. He had picked up a bottle of fine wine, because father had always insisted that the wine be stored in the library, who knows why, and brother began to drink from the bottle and to stare straight ahead with a look as if he were making grave decisions with full-scale consequences. I know what fine wine can do to a head and it seemed to me that this really wasn't the time for it.

"This isn't the friday when jesus died," I said severely.

"And how does mister skirt know that?" he snarled, thinking it would floor me.

"All right, first of all, where is the billy goat? The friday when jesus died always comes at the time of year when the ice starts to melt on the pond."

Saying that, I repeated to myself for the nth time that it couldn't be a gift from god to have to die like that on a fixed date every year. If it were me, anyway, when my turn came I wouldn't beat around the bush, I'd kick the bucket in one shot, like papa.

My brother shrugged to show that he didn't give a fly fart. I longed to tell him that this was no time to be rolling on the floor with laughter like a pig, the way we always did following father's example when we got into the fine wine, but he said this thing to me that had an effect on me after all, do you know what he said to me?

"You take your inflations and scram!"

You take your inflations and scram, those are the tender words to which my brother had accustomed me — he who was, before I met you, the only being on earth the little goat had ever tried to be in love with. But with him, well, I didn't have even a demi-urge for him to stretch out on my back, it's not because he didn't have that in mind if you see what I mean. Sometimes I think that keeping your balls means assuming you can do whatever you want, drive away what's natural and it comes back as horror. Humph. But perhaps the dictionaries of chivalry have got me all worked up, have made me expect too much of the kind of love that's possible here below on our estate.

I left my brother to the sinister secret meeting he was having with himself. I equipped myself with an oil lamp and I and my inflations scrammed. I crossed the corridors, trying to get a reading on the state of the universe. I'd brought along the book of spells. I knew I should catapult myself into this book as quickly as possible and recount all the fantasic and wonderful things that had been happening to my brother and me since dawn, but my head was spinning in the wrong direction, I hadn't eaten a bite all day except for certain herbs, friendly mushrooms, and a few flowers past their prime that I'd picked going and coming along the road through the pine grove, maybe I've forgotten to mention that, they allow me to get by. Usually I need nothing more to sustain me until nightfall, along with a crumb of stoneloaf, but the day had been draining, I felt slightly askew in my body and I promised it that before daybreak I would force myself to down two potatoes. The body is an abyss, everything inside it is pitch-black.

Unquestionably the portrait gallery had suffered the least damage from the almighty mildew. The pictures were held up by frames that hung on the walls, there must have been more than twice the ten fingers of my hands. Some of them I liked very much, ones that showed landscapes impossible to imagine, so little did they resemble what I'd known hitherto on this planet of old mountains. There were also some pictures of very serious individuals who all seemed to look like one another, as if they were all the same and only their costumes changed, with the same nose, really, on all of them, and under each you could read a different name, and dates that made no sense, they went back so far compared with the dates written in our book of spells, but always there was this inscription under each of the portraits: soissons de coëtherlant. There were sluts too and blessed virgins who were called marquises, if I understood correctly, and then there were countesses, and it seems that in all likelihood I too am a soissons slut, the clarity of it suddenly sprang to my mind like a tiger, what a lot of words, thought I, I could have been in the memoirs of saint-simon.

Horse was following me and lingering in front of certain pictures, perplexed or disenchanted. Incidentally I don't know what age horse may have reached in his lifetime. We think we know certain beings and we don't even know their expiration date. From all appearances papa had kneaded him long before he kneaded my brother and me, assuming that he actually did knead him, perhaps father and horse had been together from the beginning of eternity, like correlative modes that express the same essence, if we're to rely on ethics. But those are merely suppositions and their kind and they're all tangled up with religion. Before I vacated the portrait gallery I bent down because there was something on the floor that I'd never seen before and it intrigued me. It was nothing. The desiccated cadaver of a raccoon, its paw caught in a speedtrap.

And I nearly took a nose-dive when I caught my foot in

its private parts, I mean the chains. Let me explain. Underneath the north door of the portrait gallery some chains had been screwed to the hinges in such a way that one could, should one wish, attach someone there with arms outstretched and legs wide apart. The person thus chained at the ankles and wrists would resemble an x, if you want to call a spade a spade. And that person was papa. Now and then he would order us to chain him up like that, and there's more. At the same time kid brother was required to push against father's back with his full weight so as to stretch out his arms and legs to the maximum, which can't have been good for him at his age, I don't think, to judge by the cracking. And then, at the maximum point of muscular elongation, if that's the proper term, I had to position myself in front of him and flog his naked belly with a wet rag. You could hear peculiar sounds in his chest, I hated that, and I always cried when papa forced us to do this to him. Then he would beg us to unfasten him but we weren't supposed to, and that was how he tortured us. Since he had ordered us not to take him down till nightfall we had to wait for night to take him down, never mind his pleas, his order had been categorical. Our filial duty required us to respect his instructions, watch out for whacks. Hanging from his chains like that, papa shouted insults at the arrogant individuals who stood there framed in their portraits in the gallery, and I still can't say what they could have done to him to incur his benedictions that way but they quite clearly didn't give a fly fart. I took pity though, and my tears mingled with my fragrant hair. My father did such eccentric exercises. And to think we won't see their like again.

Once past that door, I was on a vast mirrored plain and there my gaze inevitably fell far away towards the worst spot on the estate, to which we were forbidden access during father's lifetime but where I went as many times as possible, especially at night when I bore the weight of melancholy. It was a room so enormous that two hundred neighbours could have flapped their elbows, as brother and I liked to do to imitate hens, without their elbows touching, believe me if you want but you can check, it's historic. My brother had a hellish fear of going there because there was always a murmur in the air, especially in the evening, a murmur I'll say more about later, and my brother is a cretin in case you haven't realized that yet. Nothing could be less like the poor kitchen lined with planks where we spent the bulk of our earthly life than this hall filled with marble, fireplace mantels, chandeliers, paned windows as high as three little goats standing on each others' heads. Yes, chandeliers that hung from the ceiling and were shaped like strawberries, with crystal eyes and globes where the light got trapped and danced and laughed cheerily, really, things were moving on all sides, and with a little luck and a little wind which would come in through the broken windowpanes, all this was accompanied by a merry clinking as crystal-clear as a fish. But other chandeliers had fallen to the floor like overripe fruit, they had crashed to the cracked marble slabs in bunches and it made you think of some disembowelled fly, its guts full of eggs — corruption! do your duty now. And I want you to know, there was also a huge grand camel with a wing and you could have easily locked up three dead men inside it. I say wing but I don't actually know what it's called, it's a kind of table and all camels have one, to go by the illustrations, but on ours it was always standing up like an open grave, and since there was a decrepit-looking wound on the ceiling above it, whenever it rained very hard the rainwater fell inside, onto the taut strings, and made lugubrious sounds and it could have been chopin, I'm choosing my words carefully. I often stepped up to it, with respect and circumspection, because that big black piece of furniture has always seemed to me like something mysteriously alive, recalcitrant and untamed, and I would run my hand fearfully over the white keys of the keyboard, which were yellow like horse's teeth. I would have liked to hear it speak to me, to hear its true voice from the deep when it sang, perhaps it wouldn't have been lugubrious at all if anyone had deigned to caress it, following my example so to speak, but papa never ever made music on the grand camel, don't ask me why, yet papa had music in his very dick.

All that was in daytime, because at night, I'll tell you about that in a moment, it was magnificent, but first I have to tell you about the silverware, that was during the daytime too. It was lined up in big cupboards set into the walls, which stood three times the height of the little goat and rose all the way to the ceiling, so I had to use a stepladder, and they had panels of glass in beautiful bright colours, all jack-knife dives and leaps, and that's why it had been sheltered from the ambient mildew, the silverware I mean. I had parties there sometimes on days of miraculous circumstances, when all at the same time the sun was shining, father had trotted to the village, and my brother was far away at the other end of the estate playing with his balls. You can't imagine how many there were, it took me four hours just to spread them out, I'm still talking about the silverware obviously. I don't know if I've thought to write it down but cleanliness makes me crazy in my head I love it so much. There were spoons of every kind, of every family, and saucers and plates and cups and knives, it would never end if I listed everything that was stuck away in the drawers and cupboards of the ballroom, in gold, in crystal, in silver, in bristol glass, in philosopher's stone, in all the most wonderful things you can imagine. I studied each utensil, that's the proper term, I wouldn't tolerate the slightest fog, everything had to sparkle, I polished, I germaned, never has my skirt been used so much or for a better purpose. I removed the dust and debris from the marble strewn on the ground, that verb strew again, and I arranged my manikins of light with a thousand and one loving attentions under the tallest of the windows where the sun came in to dance in this wonderful labyrinth of cleanliness and sparkling bones. I think those utensils, there were a good forty-hundred and fifty-thirteen of them, every time I tried to count them as I lined them up in rows my head began to spin in the wrong direction and I'd lose track of the number, there were so many, cross my heart. Sometimes I would waltz all around them, my bare feet on the chilly battered slabs. But mostly I stood and gazed at them with my arms stretched out like a sparrow, as still as a frightened mouse, and I felt all the sorrows and bereftments drop from my wings like the icicle stalactites that fall from the roofs in the spring, that father in his lifetime called tsoulalas because he'd been a missionary in japan when he was a fine-looking lad, don't ask me where that is, it's somewhere on the other side of the pine grove.

BUT THE STRANGEST THING in the ballroom was at night, as I'm about to prove through my memories. Papa, you know what he's like, on the nights when he cried as he looked at the daguerreotypes, that's the right word, my brother and I could do whatever we wanted, except start fires, obviously. I mean, someone could have set off flour-crackers on his right, where pascal had an abyss, and papa wouldn't have taken his eyes off the tears falling one by one from the tip of his nose onto his speckled wrists, I think that was one of his exercises. I took advantage of it to escape to the ballroom. Obedience to the truth forces me to say that getting there after dark required one to cross through a slice of night, because the kitchen of our earthly abode, which faced the fallow fields near the library and the portrait gallery, was made all of planks and logs, which with our tottering help father had conceived and built with his own hands and ours a golden age ago, I believe it was back when I still had the whole kaboodle between my thighs, the kitchen as I say was about sixty legs from the outbuildings behind the towers where the ballroom lay. You also had to cross through the pig wallow by fording the sleeping beasts, because we had a wallow too, I don't know if the notion of writing that down has entered my head. Quite often, if we'd been able to extricate ourselves from the wallow, we had to walk through dead hens for a dozen legs. As for the stables, we'll say no more about them, it had been a day of yore since anyone had moved in there and horse wouldn't be the one to venture inside, take my word, you'd have needed cannons just to get the doors open.

From this distance, if we turned around we couldn't see the kitchen of our earthly abode even in daylight, so negligible was it, tucked away between the monumental library and the portrait gallery. I was taking a little break in the flower pavilion, so named because quantities of friendly weeds grew there in disorder and delirium. A balcony, too, where I used to go, was hung up above like a drum and it stretched out into a promontory above the quagmires, and you could see far, far away. The pine grove went on and on, as far as the eye could see. And the mountains and the grey sky. Some evenings at dusk the horizon was so clear that I felt as if I were going to fall into it, all the way down to the other side of the world, and I'd turn my head for fear that it would start spinning in the wrong direction.

Finally, the manor house. It still had a certain look about it and it could have housed an army plus three emperors with their retinue. Only pigeons and sparrows lodged there now and they were constantly squabbling, inspired by the hens. Two wings extended it in a horseshoe and at the tips of these wings were the towers, as I've written. To all that were attached the outbuildings, of which no more mention will be made, to do them justice you'd need to hire a specialist in heraldry or trigonometry and I have my flaws but not those. Nonetheless I will say that if you drew a straight line on either end of the horseshoe, the famous ballroom was located where the two met, about twenty legs away, and it's high time I talked about what went on there at night.

I arrived and settled in discreetly so as not to disturb the shadows, which I'll say more about later, on the crates where papa piled the ingots, and it may be because of those ingots, in fact, that papa flatly forbade us to set foot in the room. First I aligned my eyes with the back of the room and the big flaking mirror, I mean it was covered with patches of verdigris scale. It no longer reflected colours, which is the fate of sick mirrors. Everything was cast back in black and white and ash, with a dry taste of bygone days. It could have been a mirror that had stopped the way a clock does, that reflected not the present nowadays time of the room but faces from the most distant memory, like when death wins out over life, believe me if you can, and this is why.

Once I had spent a long time staring at the mirror, on condition that I didn't look away, the aforementioned murmur began to rise, and it was a murmur of murmuring, of scraps of remote laughter, of rustling silk, of fans that opened with a twitch of the wrist, of the dreams of birds as they rub their wings against their prison bars. One time I brought my brother there to be sure my head wasn't playing tricks on me, but what do you think? No sooner did the murmuring start than he was quivering like jelly, and then he left the ends of his tether all over the place. I stayed there by myself. Too bad for cretins. I'm not afraid of things that turn out the wrong way and interfere with the everyday matters of this world, it's a change from the pervading decrepitude and the way all things insist on wearing down, if that's what I'm trying to say.

And then figures would begin to appear in the convalescent mirror. A hubbub of faces, with the tumult slowly rising. And gowns of velvet and velasquez, and wigs, and cavaliers in magpie-tail coats if there is such a thing, and the throng started to overflow the mirror into the room, which filled up and was taken over by them. No doubt this will surprise you but, as the figures took shape around me, behind me and on my right and on my left, I had the impression that I myself was becoming unreal, I mean little by little I was becoming invisible, I looked at my hands and I could see the battered marble floor right through them. Soon I no longer existed. I was merely the memory of that ball from another time and I want to tell you, it felt as if it were all part of my own most distant childhood, if I had one. At the heart of the crowd I could sense the arms of a slut around me, or a blessed virgin, who smelled sweet and was bending over to say things into my ear while she laughed gentle laughter, even if I no longer existed. And it also seems to me that, without my seeing him, papa too was nearby. God but that slut, if she was one, smelled good and tender and fresh, like a bouquet of wild roses. And there at the very end I could see coming towards me a bambino who was laughing too, and I had the very clear sensation that this bambino's face was the same as mine, with the same laughter, though she wasn't me we were like two bubbles. I don't know if I'm making myself understood but I need only close my eyes to see it again, as clear as rock crystal, inside my bonnet. Then the throng dissipated, the murmur disappeared, I was there all alone and amazed and surrounded by a fern-like silence that the wind, coming in through the windowpanes, pierced with remnants of murmurs and with soft hissing sounds.

I was rememorying all that, thinking that I might have to go back to the ballroom one last time before disaster swept us away, as I went from the mirrored plain in the portrait gallery to the kitchen of our earthly abode. I held the lamp in one hand and the book of spells in the other, having in mind to watch over father for even the shortest length of time despite the fact that it was late. Look, you'll tell me these are just details but I am recording the facts with probity and simplicity. When we laid father's mortal remains on the table this morning, and I remember this very clearly, his palms were turned down towards the ground with the fingers slightly curled, like someone with vertigo who clutches the grass while looking at the sky because he's afraid of falling all the way up to the very heights of the unroving stars. Those hands were in the same position when brother tried to hack papa to pieces, I remember noticing it anew. Now, though, papa's palms were turned skywards with the fingers unfolded, as if he were receiving the stigmata et cetera, I'm saying it as it is. To which I would add that he was now as hairless as a melon, his lip glabrous, no moustache or lambchops, that's what I would call nothing and shoo. To be my father's son you need to have a tough hide and not be afraid of surprises, that's what I was trying to get at.

BEFORE I ENCOUNTERED the ethics of spinoza, which I don't understand a tickle of and which could set dresses on fire, I asked myself a quantity of questions that, now I'm enlightened, strike me as very futile and pitiful, but they came back to my mind in spite of myself when I was watching over father's astonishing mortal remains, trying to get a bearing on our situation in the universe. I wondered what would become of us, particularly me. If it should happen that we could no longer live on our land, where the devil would we go, I ask you? And in that case would my brother and I be taken to the same place or would we, on the contrary, be separated from one another forever, a prospect that made my head spin in the wrong direction so much that I had to press my palms against my chair to avoid falling to the floor, pulled down by the weight of my inflations. Or maybe they'd decide to bury us at the same time as papa, who knows, and maybe they would make us expire beforehand so they could do so, it's only human, and then I wondered about the means they would employ to make my brother and me pass as mortal remains from the state of apprentice to that of full-fledged journeyman, if you get my drift.

And that was when all sorts of questions swept back into my mind that I used to ask myself before I read the ultra-incomprehensible ethics of spinoza, where as recently as last year I learned, among other things, that true religion is not a meditation on death but a meditation on life — corruption! do your duty. Actually that was one of father's sayings, that our job was to try to understand, just as the job of porridge is to be porridge, I don't know if you see the logic. Let me explain. When I was a little goat even smaller than the one I am now, I sometimes wondered, since we knew we were mortal, whether after brother and I became cadavers in due course we would make our way to paradise, purgatory, or hell, after the age for limbo there were no other possibilities. I'd reached the conclusion that in purgatory they make people think they're in hell. Which is enough, as I see it. No need to suffer eternally if we've already suffered by thinking for even one minute that this suffering will be eternal, of course. As for hell, I never declared that it doesn't exist, but the harshest punishment inflicted on the devil, I tried to persuade myself, is that god doesn't send anyone there, because the devil is vain and jealous like my brother, which is something that deserves to be punished, holy mother, and that's precisely what I was worried about for kid brother, should it turn out that the author of our days did indeed hurl people down below following a decision that was in any case irrevocable. I thought to myself: "Poor devil." Yet there was no shortage of his efforts here below, if I'm to judge by my own time here.

All that, as I was saying, was before spinozan ethics spattered me with light, inasmuch as it teaches one to puff up with haughtiness in the face of these superstitions that are only good for making low-grade noggins tremble. But faced with the fait accompli of papa's corpse, I confess that I was no longer sure of anything. I suppose the prospect of the sly devils in the village forcing my brother and me to kick the bucket without even uncting us extremely skewered me in every direction on the barbecue grill of those ancient queries on the matter of hell and its kind. Ah la la, all these things one has to keep together in one's head, at all times. But the earth would be a dull place if no one asked any questions about it.

I was sitting facing the body, in a wicked chair that was the chair where papa liked to sit when he treated himself to a stoppit. I sat there with my shoulders very straight and my back like a rod, in the posture prescribed for countesses, according to my own fine education. I was still holding the oil lamp in my right hand and the book of spells in my left, the hand connected to the heart, and the base of the lamp was resting on my knee. I heard stirrings in the dim dark at my side but I was used to them, our estate is a veritable gold mine for little creatures, we leave rot and corruption lying around everywhere. Still, I told myself, papa's mortal remains are a grand thing. A considerable event, of interest to the universe in its pensive totality. His remains cast their shadow over our lives, my brother's and mine, that's the least I can say, but the shadow also extended far beyond, all the way to the land that's called holy, if such a thing exists. And what would befall the planet, as well as the neighbours who swarmed upon it? Would they be gripped by a rage of despair and pain on learning the news, would they hurl bombs everywhere, as it is written, and burn everything, smash everything, tear out their eyes and the hair around their hole, the one where we were going to bury the body? Would god himself descend into our fields, fretful and unshaven? Would the forests perish as well? And so forth? All this was spinning in my bonnet like the wings of a mill.

When father existed on this side of things, at least the life of the world had a meaning, twisted and bumpy though it may have been, that's the point I'm trying to make. The inexorable course of the stars and the path of the galaxies, the vegetables that obstinately grow beneath the hairy earth, even the little creatures that scurry so softly through the thickets and the odours they send up from the dense grasses, all of it had a direction, though it didn't show, a direction that papa's orders had stamped on them. Now that he was defunct, it was as if a gigantic gust of wind had swept the earth with just one blast and had left nothing standing. I don't know if I'm making myself understood, and that has me worried sick. I've been feeling very insecure, you might say, ever since I've been using the gender of pronouns to call myself a slut.

But what would befall the Fair Punishment, that was what was bothering me most in life as I faced the mortal remains. How I became aware of it, of the Fair I mean, you'll think I'm inventing the wheel but it happened the way I'm about to tell you. Once upon a time, long before I became a natural source of blood, I most likely still had the whole kaboodle on my bum, as religion would have it, I'd watch my father at night when he thought my brother and I had sunk into the nothingness of sleep. He would go to the woodshed, also known as the vault, and spend long hours there. You mustn't judge my father only by the whacks, he had something under his breast, I mean inside his chest, as you'll soon be convinced. He brought along the oil lamp, because at nighttime the vault is the realm of darkness, and dangerous too because of everything strewn there and its opposite. At the time I was already in the habit of shoulder blades in the tall grass, of all night long under the stars, that is, with my hair spread all around me in the chilly beads of dew, to say nothing of the emerald mosquitoes, with whom I've always been on excellent terms, or all the small creatures that avoided me, scurrying quietly away so as not to disturb my bad dreams. And as father crossed the playing fields he sometimes came so close he nearly stepped on me, but he was sunk so deep inside his own dark thoughts that he didn't even notice me buried there in the grass, humph. Without going so far as to get my navel in a knot, I'd never had even a tickle of curiosity about him, and meddling in what was none of my business, I mean trying to find out what kept papa busy in the vault for hours at a time, had never been my strong point, up until the night when all at once my ear pricked up. I have to say that I was a little askew in my sleep, where I still sometimes talk, walk, take part in this or that activity and have no awareness of it in my bonnet, even write, write things that greatly surprise me the next day. Now on the night in question, somnambulistically, as it's called, I'd shifted a few legs away from the place in the field where I customarily abandoned myself to the restorative void, so that my ear was three toad-leaps from the shed door, that's what I'm trying to tell you. Having heard a murmur of tears, I got up and, with at least a quarter of my head still in orbit, I approached the basement window of the vault, and that's not all. Father was there on his knees, crying, his forehead pressed against the glass box which I was seeing for the first time, true as I'm, and there I was running hell-bent for leather down the endless slope of fascination that would endure for a great many seasons yet to come.

For the first time, because I have to note that, apart from certain well-defined categories of objects in this world, I have very little interest in the vanities here below and it had never crossed my mind that anything in that woodshed might have significance for me, so I'd never come closer to it than four or five legs, as is true after all for a quantity of other outbuildings on our estate, so how was I supposed to know what was inside, including the Fair Punishment?

Which I was seeing then for the first time in my bitch of a. Before that day, if anyone had told me that papa had the slightest interest in flowers, I'd have mulled it over and over inside my head and I wouldn't have believed it. But papa was there several times a week, quite unaware of my presence on the other side of the basement window, and he was scattering petals all around the glass box and murmuring as if he were talking to neighbours like you and me. My father had always been old for as long as I've known him, so old that I only think of fantasies when I try to picture him otherwise, such as back when he was a fine-looking lad in a soutane in japan. I would hear him crying more in the years to come, and more and more often, but when I saw him in tears like that for the first time, as old as the mountains and talking to a glass box as if it were perfectly normal, I had the same feeling, astonished and bereft, that I'd have had if I'd suddenly seen a drop of blood stand out on an old dry stone, cross my heart. I don't know if I'm making myself understood.

In any event, with the passing seasons it became a kind of secret mass for me, one I attended by myself, unbeknownst even to the priest who was officiating in the vault. Obviously I didn't want him to know I was there, because of the whacks and their kind, which I could already picture, and when he was about to finish and leave the shed at the first languors of dawn I took my legs and my heels and we all decamped, whoosh, evanescent and silent as my friend the dragonfly. What's more, it had become easy for me to anticipate the moment when papa would be finished, you can be sure of that. When all was said and done, this priest's *ite missa est*, if I may put it that way, consisted of caring for the Fair Punishment, dusting it off with great care, changing its wrappings, shifting it cautiously, then gently putting it back in its low box.

And one time when papa came out again, I don't know what was going through my noggin but I was planted there in front of the door, and he had an attack of surprise at the sight of me. He raised his hand and I my elbow in front of my cheek, thinking I'd be contending with you know what, but contrary to all expectations his palm settled gently onto my skull and he said in a voice that was tight but tranquil, as he pointed inside the vault: "It's a fair punishment," whence its name, which has stayed with me.

And that was how the Fair and everything inside the vault became familiar to me, I often went there with papa, those memories are sacred. I helped him look after the glass box, I even got to be on first-name terms with it, talking to it as if it were a full-fledged neighbour the way papa did, like a truly deranged noggin. Finally we would extirpate the Fair Punishment from its box, unless we'd left it out the time before, that happened too, and we would dust it with our gazes. Afterwards it was not uncommon for us to spend long hours sitting there in silence, holding hands, my father and I, as true as I'm, those memories are sacred. It's strange what happened inside me then, I want you to know that. I had the impression that rememories were coming back to me of a time when nothing on our blasted estate was as it is nowadays. First of all, the sun: it was everywhere. And it was always following me, as sure as I'm suffering. I would fling myself here and here, and there it was clinging to my heels and souls, ah la la, it was tiring in the end, not to mention that it shined my eyes. The moon was the same. I'd go to the other end of my legs, if that's how you say it, then I'd play at retracing my footsteps, and pop! There it was again, between the summits of the trees, even though I'd been running. Even today. I sometimes think that I'm not just anyone after all, living as I do with two stars on my buttocks. Same problem with the pompom clouds. Tss.

And it also seems to me — to go back to that unthinkable time, the time I dreamed about when I was holding my father's hand in the vault — that back then my size didn't even come up to papa's knee-bone; he seemed as high as a wall to me, and always laughing and smiling, as if it were possible that at a certain era in my life I'd had two little wings on my back, bambino-style. And always accompanying this vision, this picture of a slut, if that's what she was, who smelled as good and fresh and tender as the wild roses along the edge of the pine grove. I have an even clearer imagination from that period when I didn't come up to my father's knee, which is this. There was a cherub at my side and she wasn't me but we were as much alike as two bubbles, from as brother keeps trying to convince me, and papa had a magnificat glass in his hands, that's what it's called, and through the power of magic that magnificat glass allowed him to capture the rays of the sun, which made black lines accompanied by little curls of smoke when they landed on a wooden plank. Papa smiled as he formed letters with those concentrated lines of lightning, but I'll have more to say about that small plank at the proper time, and you'll see why.

To finish with these memories, if that's what they are, I'll tell you that they agitated me for a long time, especially during my dreams and again last winter when kid brother was trying to persuade me, against all reason, that we had a small sister somewhere in the mountains god knows where, a discussion that I very clearly remember having already brought up elsewhere. But in the end it didn't stop me from sleeping, it was too bothersome. I would shrug a shoulder, I'd flick some blood at him if I had some. And the rest of the time, I mean when papa and I weren't in the woodshed, papa was as usual — taciturn as the billy goat when he comes to us in spring, deep inside his bonnet of dark thoughts, commanding everything from the bedroom upstairs as he'd done just the day before.

As for my brother, it's as if he just has an idea of the Fair Punishment's existence, it scared him so badly he pleated his pants; I think he bad-dreams about it still.

But, well, I was there facing papa's mortal remains and rememorying all that, pointlessly of course, because I wish someone would tell me what use memory is. I'll try my best to put those things into a corner and not think about them any more, and instead to reflect through understanding, as ethics teaches us. I gathered my ideas together so as to get a bearing on the present state of the universe regarding my brother and me. Father had become nothing more and nothing less than a thing, because there was no one inside now, and I felt that even this thing with nothing inside no longer belonged to us. Hordes would come to us from the village, ignorant of our customs, respecting nothing, understanding even less, frothing at the snout, agitated and stupid as flies, and they would dispossess us completely: of our estate, my dictionaries, the Fair Punishment too, quite likely, and consequently of the power of speech and of the very mortal remains of papa, which they'd bury where they saw fit, in the dung and the mud.

What was cruel was that even if they left my brother and me in peace, we were no further ahead. Had we continued to respect father's rules, to repeat the rosary of his deeds after a fashion, we'd have only agitated the void, if you want my opinion, because outside the living body of papa those rites made no sense whatsoever, and all the fragile meanings I'd up till now hung here and there on the great remnants of the world, the way I saw bambinos hanging christmas-coloured balls on a fir tree in my illustrations, I watched them shatter one by one in little puffs, in the manner of soap foam, from the mere fact of my father's awe-inspiring death. Which filled a gap on the "horizon-of-our-life."

I'll have you know, though I don't dare admit it, the temptation was strong to let myself be pushed around, to give up, to wait for our neighbours to arrive and submit to their sticks, because my brother and I no longer had any code or law to oppose theirs. I forbade myself to dream that a handsome cavalier would come and take me in his arms and carry me away on his white horse to bounteous lands, above all I tried not to think that the handsome cavalier would have your smile and your eyes and your brackmard sword gleaming like a spoon.

I sensed that my only chance, if that's the correct term, was to bear witness, and I took my courage in both hands, that is to say, my book of spells and my pencil, and I traced this first sentence with tears stinging my eyes: *We had to take the universe in hand, my brother and I, for one morning just before dawn . . .* — or something close to that, because I was short of time, I was short of everything — so that I could read myself over again.

I DON'T KNOW HOW LONG I was able to write at top speed and with my heart pounding the pavement, because there was no moon and the sky was covered with limbo, but I must have filled a dozen pages at one go without stopping, speeding through sentences and words like a bullet through the pages of a bible. When the secretarious got it into her head to pedal through the words, clear the tracks, it's coming fast, strewth, at a speed that can break necks. I was interrupted by a sound my stomach made, it's called a gargoyle if I remember correctly, and all at once I recalled the vow I'd made to my reluctant bird-belly to eat a potato or two before dawn, which I hadn't kept. As I closed the book of spells it seemed to me that papa's knees had moved. His legs had been as stiff and straight as sticks when we took him down from his miserable mast this morning, and now they were slightly bent, like a dead spider's. But we'd finally got to where we were. To ease my conscience, I should note here that his bare feet strangely resembled two mouldy loaves of bread, in shape as well as in colour. We're not much in the eyes of death, either before or after, that's a news flash from yours truly.

From among the scattered sacks I plucked a potato and also a beet I'd encountered before, I went to the bucket to wash them and then I wiped them with the saturn ring of my skirt. A third of the beet, which was already soft, had been gnawed away. Beets are like us, and so are the rats that gnaw them. Whether they're devoured or left to rot, they won't stick around very long here below, not for anybody, and don't try to tell me otherwise. I crouched under the table where father was and began to chew. I had picked up the book of spells, and as I went on writing with a mighty hand and an outstretched arm the strangest sounds could be heard from upstairs. Horse, who was lying on the floor not far from me, sat up on his feet and looked at me with his walleyed gaze. A commotion of panic, of racing feet coming from all the bedrooms. It seemed to be heading for the veranda, which served as a belvedere and gave onto the bedroom where papa et cetera just the day before. Alarmed and in the grip of an evil omen, I huddled around the friendly book of spells. Brother burst in noisily from the staircase. He sped to the cupboard, knocking over everything in his way, and in a spurt of impatient anger he reached out his arm and knocked over a chair that had committed no crime aside from being in his way, and it bounced off papa's belly. That was when I realized that brother had just been touched by grace.

"What are you doing?" I asked, not daring to emerge from beneath the table.

Brother was battling with the headgear on the nail jar, trying to unscrew it. He made an irritated gesture at me that meant, be quiet. Then went back upstairs, taking along the handsaw and the hammer. The commotion started up again, more threatening than ever. I pressed my fists over my ears, I thought I was screaming. What I wanted to do was leave then and there, flee to the village and throw myself at the feet of the sly devils, so fed up was I at that moment with brother, with corpses, with burials and I don't know what all — with a life as black as soot. But I couldn't abandon kid brother. I felt perplexedly that just now he was tumbling down a slippery slope hell-bent for leather, and that I ought to fling myself across his path like a chair to stop him, to say the least about the way things looked to me. So I went upstairs in my turn, using the staircase where, just this morning, papa had exited like a piano.

The halves! I never knew where they'd come from, but do we ever know where anything whatsoever comes to us from on this blasted estate? There must have been almost as many of them as there were portraits in the portrait gallery, and I'd been quite fond of them for a day of yore. Often I would deck them out, bah, in this and that, but always prettily, and I behaved with them as if we were with saint-simon at the court of the sun king, abounding in handsome cavaliers and counts in their dreamy outfits and tales of chivalry that were like visions, as you can imagine, and in the secrecy of my heart, so much was I my father's son that I pretended to be their countess. We called them halves because they had only a body, made of wax and wood. They lacked the portion of their insides that allows one to suffer and so to call oneself a full-fledged neighbour, if I'm making myself clear. We can also name them dummies, that's allowed, although it's not as strong and not as accurate, and you don't do speech any favour to associate with words that rattle around in your sleeve after the handshake.

Brother had lined them up on the belvedere, along the railing, and plunked them onto seats. One had a broom in its hands, one had a big piece of tree branch, one had a pick or a rake — at a distance you might have thought it was a guardroom, and that was what my brother had in his idea box. Never before had I seen him in such a state of exaltation, it was as if sparks were flying out his ears and out his hole.

"Brother," I said, "surely you don't expect to drive the villagers away with halves armed with broomsticks?"

Brother had lit half a dozen oil lamps which produced a glow which was hardly reminiscent of paradise, I assure you. While he was thrashing about from one end of the belvedere to the other, arming his soldiers in the aforementioned manner, at regular intervals he was gulping fine wine directly from the bottleneck. Ah la la. And then he said:

"I am the master of the estate. Let them come! I'm not

99

afraid to talk to them! I'll answer them through the asshole of my cannon!"

"Your cannon? What cannon?" I tried to reason with him. "Papa is nothing but mortal remains, his body will never move again!"

"I'm the one who is papa now!"

And he thumped his chest with pride, drumming it with his fists the way papa used to do, in the manner of gorillers.

In summer it often happened that I would try to keep a straight face while telling a butterfly that had been standing for half a turn of the clock on the summit of my knee: "I am your master," just to see, but our mandibles no longer sufficed and we'd burst out laughing, I mean my friend would fly away, because just try explaining to a butterfly what it means to be master of an estate! Something even a butterfly can't understand must not be very important, as it's sometimes my opinion to think. But I hasten to add that opinions on the matter were divided in my family, I mean when papa was still breathing like one man.

Be that as it may, I left brother to his mad brain, that's the right word for it. I picked up my oil lamp and rushed to the stairs.

"Where are you going?" he howled, in a voice that sounded as if he had just been thrown naked onto burning coals.

I said nothing and ran outside to rush into the living night. I went in the direction you can imagine, towards the woodshed, also known as the vault. I knew I would be relatively safe there, since brother was cretinous about going inside, because of you know what. Leaning against the stone table where the Fair Punishment reigns, and I had to elbow it aside to make room for myself, I began to write, forging straight ahead, as is my devastating custom. I only broke off my composition to go to the door with a shudder and cast a glance at what brother was accomplishing under the tyrannical influence of grace. In a sense he hadn't failed because really, from this distance, you might have taken them for standing soldiers, the kind you can see in my dictionaries. At times he brought his hands together in a megaphone and shouted: "Let them come! I've got a few things to say to those neighbours!" I went back to my stone table, shivering and sad. How I wished I were at your side, under your protection, all tiny and terrified with admiration. But I pushed my hair back on either side of my shoulders and, sighing, I plucked up the courage of my pencil.

Two or three times, balls of fire that were pretty in their own way crossed the sky, launched from the belvedere. What he'd made them from I hadn't the slightest idea, nor did I know how he'd been able to catapult them all the way to the middle of the field. One ended up so close to the woodshed that I nearly cried out, but after due reflection I refrained. Such ingenuity in an individual with as few brains in his bonnet as my brother could only be due to a state of grace, as I've said, and no doubt it was the sudden feeling of intelligence, after years of mental darkness, that had driven his brain mad.

On top of all that, brother was striking the hammer against a long rectangle of tin and making a noise like thunder, to make people think, I suppose, that he was on first-name terms with the elements he claimed to command, but who would be taken in by that, I ask you, except himself, scattered in the wretched pieces of his mind? Humph.

Suddenly I understood that those balls of fire I'd seen against the sky were in fact marking the return of the flaming partridges that jupiter junior had made from a turpentine tree, if that's the right name for it. In any event, poor birds. The author of deeds has no pity or shame.

And so the whole night passed. I gave it the part of myself that uses words to keep going. I covered some twenty pages of paper with my minuscule, crowded writing, and shoo. By the end, my head was useless. My brain was melting through my eyes, they burned so much, and the pencil escaped from my hand and ran away.

And I'll have you know that the situation struck me as being so fenced in on every side that I reached the point where I wondered if it might not be better to follow the ariadne clew of father's rope and hang myself too, to resolve all the problems in one twinkling of an eye, that's what ropes are for, my pet. But then what would become of brother? And would I ever see you again, o my fiancé? And what a bereftment for the birds who dance with me in secrecy, even those at the other end of the earth, and my manikins of light and the wrappings of the Fair Punishment?

Dawn was beginning to point its rosy finger. I took a last look outside, because I could hear a murmuring of hammers. My brother was nailing a seat to the summit of two stepladders that he'd joined together with belts. And he was doing that at the edge of the vegetable garden, hardly a dozen legs from the house. You can check, they're still there, those accursed stepladders. It was then that I saw a shape appear at the other end of the field, along the pine grove, among the wild roses, and I couldn't make up my mind as to what it was. I believe I noted this strange apparition earlier, here in my last will and testament, when it first occurred some fifty pages ago. But I finally knew what the silhouette was in the dawn: it was nothing less than our neighbour standing on his fool's bauble, making his way across this earth by hopping like a magpie. It was the beggar.

THE MENDICANT, IF YOU WANT. He was wearing his houp-land, grimy is the word for that coat, as is neverending, and let me tell you, we sorely needed that in the midst of this turmoil, ah la la. As he drew near he was travelling at his affluent senator's pace. He would sometimes interrupt the rhythm of his cane, which might have been called a happy leg drunk on independence and liberty, to stand on his central joystick, which was faithfully present at every step of his rendezvous with the grass and the hard-packed earth, and like a peacock fanning his tail he spun his stick in cartwheels before setting off again, the syntax is courtesy of saint-simon. He was a neighbour in a carefree mood, our mendicant, I don't know if I remembered to note that. Those who are fretful beneath the salt of heaven don't lodge at his inn, I guarantee.

My brother gazed at him briefly, his hand suspended in midair, his eyebrows and lashes drawn together. From my hiding place I thought I could read the merest hint of hesitation and surprise, which raised my hope, but think about it, the state of grace won't be dismantled over such a small thing. Kid brother continued to tap with his hammer on the seat he intended to nail to the summit of the two stepladders, which shivered with every blow, and there I was, given over to my bereftment.

The beggar planted his joystick in the middle of the field and, hooking his cane over his forearm, began to clap his hands and laugh, apparently dumbfounded by my brother's cabinetmaking prowess. Likewise, when he spied the belvedere and the halves armed with brooms and mops, his mouth went oh. It made him slap his thigh, and noises came from his throat like the ones dogs make, which are his means of expression, as I've written before. Then as he drew nearer he knocked his knuckles on the left-hand stepladder, the way you might knock on a door, to attract kid brother's attention, at which he succeeded. He put his well-named index finger beneath his nostrils to mimic a moustache, by which he meant that he was wondering where father was. Brother's only reply was to drop his head to one side, close his eyes, stick out his tongue, and, with his free hand, make as if he were holding an imaginary rope above his head, attempting thereby to resemble a hanged man, there was no mistaking it. At first, stupor from the beggar. Who finally decided that this was a good one, and he was in a wonderful mood as he made his way towards the vault where I already was, unbeknownst to him or to kid brother. He sat against the wall. And then devoted himself to gazing at kid brother as if he were the whole show, in the manner of our only toy. As he did so, he made a little music with his mouth, the beggar did, prroo poo-poo, if you see what I mean, comparable to the sound horse made when he was snorting with his chops, and that reminded me, where could he have got to, horse that is, he seemed to have disappeared into nowhere. Then the beggar took a corruption sandwich from his pocket and bit into it with no fuss or complexes. As for kid brother, when he'd finished he perched himself at the very summit of the stepladders, with a feather standing in for a sceptre, and the desiccated raccoon corpse I'd seen in the portrait gallery a few hours earlier, which he'd plunked onto his head, by way of a crown. Like a raining king, he took his place on the throne. The beggar applauded.

Oh how I didn't want to succumb to sleep, I wanted to finish my last will and testament before disaster ensued. But I was abandoned by my strength, it had taken off like a pencil. Whatever we do and however it may be and no matter how far we go, at the end of the day we have to lie down and sleep, it's inevitable. There's a leash around our necks, the fatigue that holds us to the earth finally pulls us to it and we fall, always, that's the way it is. It's the elastic of death.

I was wakened by a detonation. I couldn't have slept for more than one half-circle of the clock, for the day was still languishing. The little goat was so confused in her noggin that as I was going to the door I stumbled over all kinds of trash, I even opened the skin on my leg, on the plough I think, a stinging pain and it started to bleed too. But anyway, at the point I'd reached.

The detonation came from the fact that my brother had unearthed a muskrat god knows where and he'd loaded it, you could still see a bit of blue smoke floating at one end of it, like papa's mouth when he belched a hot pepper. I was aware that brother knew things about our estate that I didn't know, because there were outbuildings where I never ventured but where he would spend long days. As for me, as long as there were wild roses to gather, and friendly mushrooms and my daily ration of dictionaries and my manikins of light and my silverware, I had very little curiosity about the vanities here below, to which religion invites us, as I think I've noted earlier. Kid brother had undoubtedly known of the muskrat's existence for a long time, and as I watched him I was beginning to understand certain things I hadn't attached much importance to before. You see, whenever papa went to the village I would hear similar detonations now and then, at the time I'd told myself it must be branches suddenly breaking — because of the wind or the accumulated freezing rain, because in our part of the world freezing rain accumulates from year to year, spanning all the summers, what can I tell you, so as far as I was concerned the sound it made was just like that. It was coming back to me now that at such times I'd never known where brother was, and now I suspect that he must have gone to get his muskrat and fire it at the partridges. Because — and this too suddenly appeared very clearly in my memory — it was on those very days when I heard the detonations that brother claimed he'd found two dead birds along the roadside, and what's more, he cooked them and ate them with papa, ugh. I never ate any, as you can imagine. I'd have vomited my insides out if anyone had obliged me to put pieces of boiled partridge corpse in my mouth, and I was crying inside as I watched them eat, though it didn't show. Oh blast, it isn't muskrat I wanted to write, it's musket. God how tired my poor head is sometimes, I forget the meanings of words, which are all I have. Even musket isn't exactly the correct term, if such a thing exists. I think I should have said rifle. Ah la la. And my brother fired again in the direction of the pine grove. I don't know if there was something over there that he wanted to put to death, and if so, what, but the recoil was so powerful that brother landed on his hole. Which made him laugh. He got up, a little unsteady on his supports. He picked up a bottle of fine wine and drank from it, throwing his head back like a real pig, but then, slightly embarrassed, he realized that it was empty and threw it nonchalantly against the stone wall, where it burst into smithereens, as I feared my own skull would go flying.

Now that the day had nearly dawned, it was clear that the bodyguard on the belvedere was only halves, and that nothing about the throne brother had made for himself with the help of the two stepladders would impress anybody, I swear, beginning with myself. I watched, shaking my head with exasperation. At this point I saw the beggar hopping along the hill, he had left my bonnet completely. Cutlery dropped from the pockets of his houpland, and he was snickering like a nasty mouse and with the hand that wasn't busy propelling him on his cane he was holding to his chest a heap of silver cups and all the rest, from the ballroom. His face was strained and radiant and at the same time his eyes gleamed and coveted lustily. He was still laughing, as you may imagine, at this unhoped-for manna from heaven. Meanwhile, the little goat went back to her last will and testament. What else could she do?

The sheets of paper were piling up, I wasn't rereading anything. I forged ahead with the means at hand, which saint-simon would call gaining the wall, but I trust words, in the end they always say what they have to say. Turn around five times with your eyes shut, and before you open them you will know that a stone you've thrown, which has taken off in you know not what direction, has finally landed on earth. So it is with words. In the end they always settle down somewhere, no matter what, which is all that counts. I don't mean that the secretarious lets herself write any old way. I mean that when she writes she lets herself go by forging ahead, which isn't the same thing. That's what inopportune little goats are like.

Soon I heard my brother calling me at the top of his lungs, and just from the way he was pronouncing his words I realized how much the fine wine had hammered his head. Immediately I hunkered down beneath the dirty window. I scarcely dared lift the tip of my nose to see what was losing its bearings outside. My brother, drunk as a young skunk, had mounted horse, who'd suddenly reappeared from out of nowhere, the sly devil, and he was genuinely pitiful. The poor beast's legs looked like pieces of branch that you press against the ground to make a bow. Under brother's weight his belly hung down so low that brother's toes were nearly scraping the pebbles. From his basset-hound look — because I know what a basset hound is, our former dog that was defunct from mothballs had been one — and from his gait, all squashed by my brother's weight, you might have thought this was a horse being transformed into sausage by the act of a wicked fairy, because not all fairies are good, I'll have you know. Every so often horse would hardly be able to move forward, either that or he'd stumble without rhyme or reason, and my brother would give him a taste of his heel in the spareribs, kid brother will fry with the devil, believe me, but there's more. The rope that I'd fastened around horse's belly like a girth the other morning was still there, and at the end of the rope, behind them, was a sack whose dimensions alone sufficed to inform me of what it contained. I saw the beggar, deaf to it all, step inside the kitchen of our earthly abode, hopping enthusiastically.

While jupiter junior went on calling me. He still wore, plunked onto his head like royal plumes, the corpse of the raccoon that had encountered death in a speedtrap.

At that very moment, a terrifying humming sound could be heard. It was approaching us slowly and I tell you, terrifying is the word, because it seemed to rise directly from the hell beneath our feet, a hell we must believe in if we don't want to be cast down there ourselves, but in fact brother has never wanted to believe in anything. Yet it was one of my father's sayings that little saint thomases end up setting fire to their dresses because they don't believe it's dangerous to play with matches.

SOMETHING THAT I COULDN'T have named but that sounded like a giant bumblebee the size of a jackass, which is very big for a bumblebee, heaved into sight, buzzing down the length of the road that runs through the pine grove and all the way to the seven seas. My brother had trouble staying upright on his steed, for horse was terrified by this crackling that sounded just like the noise you sometimes hear in the sky that's made by those strange birds papa called bearoplanes, if my memory is correct, and then brother and I would be off like a shot. When horse saw the bumblebee approaching, he pawed the ground with the means available, not much of which was left, and sometimes his knees bent and his belly bounced like a soft ball on the muddy ground to which our hearts will one day return as dust.

The bumblebee came to a halt not very far from brother and he stood facing me, though he didn't know it, in the place where I'd positioned myself. The bumblebee was actually a complicated machine such as we'd never seen on our estate, aside perhaps from the torture of my legs, I mean the pipe organ. It consisted of two wheels, that's all I can say about it, and it was mounted by a helmeted cavalier, believe that if you will, and when the cavalier got down from it the buzzing immediately fell silent, as I told you. The cavalier was dressed all in leather from head to toe, and when he doffed his helm and his goggles and tucked them firmly under his arm, my heart made the leap that frogs make when they throw themselves into the water, for it was you, my beloved, magnificent in the dark and supple radiance of your brackmard sword.

My brother said not a word, only gazed at the cavalier and his blasted steed, while shaking like a leaf in my hands.

The cavalier said: "Where is your sister?" Then, catching himself: "Your brother? Where's your brother, the one with the long skirt? Look, I don't wish you any harm. I am the mine inspector . . ."

Kid brother, terrified, continued to make no reply. After a moment's hesitation the cavalier started heading for the house. In a panicky fit of temper, brother beat horse's flanks with his heels to send him into a gallop, but it was too much for the poor creature, he collapsed in the mud and brother tumbled over the same way.

Brother got up, not bothering to pick up his raccoon, which had rolled off when he fell, and then he vamoosed, taking to all his heels at once, trying to overtake the inspector of yours and mine. And brother climbs onto the stepladders of his throne and nearly takes a new tumble and I have to explain things very fast now and make vulgate mistakes but listen, I've said stoppits run in our family and it was true for papa and me but not for brother, though. Jupiter junior had other resources in the way the world turns. There were times, who knows why, when he'd start to be terribly frightened, he'd get shivers all over, as if he'd come down with breathing problems, he felt as if some evil beast inside him were tying knots with his insides, as if he had to do battle with his heart to keep it beating, as if et cetera and so forth, it was no laughing matter. These attacks seemed no more enjoyable than a stoppit if you want my opinion. Well, that's precisely the kind of attack my brother was having just then, as he sat on his throne in front of the mine inspector. I only hoped he wouldn't go in his pants, which sometimes happened to him in his misery because, well, after all, in your presence the countess would have been a little bit ashamed of her family.

I'm that much surer of what the mine inspector said because I noted it all in my bonnet as you were saying it, and I could see that you were speaking loudly with the intention of my hearing you too, wherever I might be.

"Listen to me, I've come as a friend, to help you. I know you can follow what I'm saying, even if it may be a little hard to understand. Perhaps I could look after things for you. I'm an engineer but also . . . Well, I want you to know that in a few hours they'll all be here. People from the village and even from other places, maybe from the government. Yesterday I met your sister, your brother if you prefer. I can't say why but I felt a great liking for her, I mean for him — my god but this is confusing. I wanted to prepare you for their arrival. And help out a little if I could. The situation is grave, you see. I've looked at the baptismal registry with the priest. Do you understand what I'm saying? There are supposed to be two girls, twins. I saw one of them yesterday. Where is the other? What happened to the other one? And your mother? Do they still live here with you?"

I pulled the woodshed door open a crack and the creak it made attracted the inspector's attention, which was what I wanted. I positioned myself on the threshold. And immediately the inspector turned in the direction of the little goat, like a gadfly heading for the only flower in the garden.

Kid brother began to scream that he was the master, and I tell you, he didn't convince anyone. You kept walking towards me without another thought for him. At the same time, in the distance I spotted the suspicious and troubled look of the beggar, who kept his eyes on you and his nose at the window of our earthly abode.

"Why are you hiding? Are you afraid of your brother?"

I sped back inside the shed without replying. But I remember that despite the circumstances I made a special effort as I walked to have my backside look like a nice person in the mine inspector's eyes. I came to a halt, still in silence, next to the Fair Punishment, as if I wanted to let you draw your own conclusions.

"What's this vault?"

It was quite dark inside the woodshed, and he grabbed hold of the oil lamp and came closer to me. All at once he turned very green around the gills. The Fair Punishment is quite a sight, I may have forgotten to mention that. I stood at his side, hands crossed over my belly as I used to do when papa made me recite the fox that laid the golden eggs. And serenely I watched the inspector. In its little heap on the floor, the Fair Punishment feebly moved a hand and then its head, in a pitiful attempt at flight or shame, as if it wanted to gain the wall, because deep down it's a little fearful. That simple motion was enough to undo one end of a wrapping though, ah la la, and I hastened to rewrap its fingers to make it presentable, and resumed my prim posture with my hands crossed over my belly. And see how stupefied he is, our mine-inspecting poet. Aha, we aren't such a sly devil now. He was staring with eyes like saucers. The Fair Punishment, covered with grey wrappings from feet to head, mimics the mummies that illustrate my dictionaries, and resembles them. All you can see of its face is the teeth, because the Fair doesn't even know what lips are, as well as the pink tip of its tongue when it eats, and its gentle eyes, so much the same colour as my own that you'd say they were the spitting image, like two bubbles. The Fair tried a little slither towards its box, where it spends the better part of its days, painfully pushing and pulling with its raglike forearms, but it will never get to shit very far from there, the poor thing has just the tick-tock and the trail to go by, and even so. In any case it couldn't travel very far because of the chain around its neck that holds it to the wall. It has a kind of bag as well, I nearly forgot to mention that, around the belly and the backside, for the times when it might want to empty its hole.

The inspector gets his voice back, though it's all little and scrawny. "That's horrible . . . it's atrocious . . . it's . . . is that your sister? Your twin sister?"

I gave my shoulders a little shrug and rolled my eyes, as if to tell him, oh my oh my, how stupid you are!

"And that?" he said again, because he hadn't seen the last of his surprises, this cavalier with the brackmard sword.

He brought the lamp closer to the glass box. You can't really say that the dress is still on this side of things, because it's rather like a coating of dried mud, and the bony remains, you need to have been warned, I think, before you can cry out what they are. But the skull still holds up, it's still of this world. Something of the teeth too, as well as the house for the eyes, the cavities where in days of yore they lived their gazing life.

"And that, is that your mother?"

I like to write down the words your mouth utters, even when they're nonsense, I feel as if I'm holding them between my thighs against my heart, your lips. I like to talk about you in both the second and the third person, flitting from one to the other the way my friend the emerald-winged dragonfly flies from bush to daffodil in summertime. If I grasped it correctly, you displayed a brief surge of anger directed at the author of our days, who is omnipotent and a master of injustice and a connoisseur of lamenting mothers. You were cursing between your teeth while you moved around the vault in circles.

"What in god's name is that horrible thing, what in god's name . . ."

The inspector had to lean against the wall with his head bowed, like a Fair. He finally raised it and gazed at me for a long time and I could tell from his eyes that he thought the universe was a very wretched thing, and more particularly me inside it. It was high time someone beneath the salt took note of it. And so I tried to explain that she is my cross and my fate, again and forever:

"She doesn't have any skin behind her wrappings, I don't think. It was the great calcination, everything underneath burned. I say she because you can say either one. We say he or she when we talk about the Fair Punishment because, on the very very rare occasions when papa talked about it, he'd get all tangled up in the gender of his pronouns and say she, and he passed that habit on to us."

You need a huge silence to hear it but sometimes a very faint lament comes from the throat of the Fair, and since there is nearly always silence in the vault we heard the faint lament being produced. I moved the bowl of stagnant water closer but the left eyelid came down as slowly as molasses. She doesn't have the gift of speech, you have to understand her, so she closes her left eye like that when she wants to say no, it's only human. I moved the stagnant water away from her teeth.

The inspector leaned over towards the Fair, circumspectly and fearfully, and no sooner did she move her little finger than he jumped back, the way my brother the cretin does at dawn when he's afraid of the bats returning to the fold above our hair, friendly though they may be.

"She can't stand up," I went on, hitching up one end of a wrapping, "it's as if her legs are a joke. But sometimes we lie down beside each other and I make a game of unwrapping her the whole length of her body, and what I see is that we're exactly the same size. From what I could understand of my father's explanations — he was never explicit about this kind of thing, with him you always had to guess, to sew little bits of sentences together — apparently the Fair burned the dead thing here at my left in the glass box, but it must have happened before brother and I were on earth for I've never had a memory of the event, if it is one. I presume they've been here, I mean the defunct and the Fair, as long as the world has existed, and now that papa has disappeared without a by-your-leave, you'll have to settle for what I've just provided by way of light on the matter."

I placed my hand on her head, smiling at her, I think, so she'd know I wasn't angry at her.

To the inspector I went on to say: "The Fair Punishment, that's what it is called. Without it, I wonder if we'd even be able to use words. That came to me once when I was thinking about it. Perhaps all the silence that fills the life of the Fair allows my brother and me to be on first-name terms with speech, especially me. I mean, it's as if the Fair had taken all the silence on herself to free us from it and enable us to speak, and what would I be without words, I ask you. Hurray for the Fair, that was a fine piece of work. Can you see? You could say this is suffering in the purest state, all wrapped up in a single package. She's like pain that doesn't belong to anyone. We don't know if there's even a hint of understanding in her bonnet. I myself would be inclined to think yes, there is, a little bit at least."

The mine inspector had something like an attack of annoyance, and he raced over to the wall and he grabbed hold of the Fair's chain, pulling harder and harder as if he wanted to yank it out of the wall, but have no fear, it held fast. The Punishment curled up even more because of being fearful deep down. As for me, I went on talking while mechanically picking specks of dust off the glass box.

"Kid brother never comes here because the Fair always gives him the fright of his life. Papa and I, on the other hand, used to spend long hours here at night. He would rest his forehead against the glass box and treat himself to tears.

Believe me if you want, I never cried, not there and not any-where else in my whole bitch of a, it seems I don't produce tears. Papa would hold his hand in mine as he wept, the syntax is courtesy of saint-simon. And then — I don't know why, it's been a golden age since then — papa stopped want-ing to come here, and I was obliged to tie a string around my finger so I wouldn't forget to feed the Punishment, who eats nothing but porridge, and dust her off and change her wrap-pings now and then the way papa taught me, such is life, they have a tendency to rot a little, they smell of medicine. At the end of his earthly time father didn't want to hear the Fair mentioned any more. When I ventured a word on the subject he'd serve me up an earbox, if you know what I mean. So I've kept on coming here all alone, especially when I was sad or if I just had a burden of melancholy. It seemed to me that there was more love in the vault than anywhere else on our whole estate, because of the way papa had spent long nights holding his hand in mine."

Of course, I'd lied to the mine-inspecting poet a little when I told you I'd never cried in my bitch of a, because there were the times when papa made us fasten him to the door in the portrait gallery with chains and forced me to flog him with a wet cloth, as well as the times when I pumped the organ with my legs or, more generally, when I was besieged by music, but I'd told the inspector that to show my inde-pendence as well as my dignity, so that he'd find me fascinating as well as intensely pretty.

The inspector closed his eyelids and shook his head with a look of pain and despondency. When he opened them again and spoke, still in the tiniest voice, it did something to me that you no longer used the carefree way of talking you'd once used for the little goat: "And what about that? Who did that to you? Your brother . . .?"

As I was wearing a big sweater, you can't get an accurate idea about my belly, but yesterday, when he was having an effect on me by holding me against him, the mine inspector must have felt it.

"Yes, I know, my belly is swollen. And the more it swells, it's been a good two seasons, the more it seems to me that the loss of my balls is scarred over now, on my body if not in my soul, which sets me apart from my brother's poor soldiers, because I haven't bled now for, soon it will be more than two seasons. My belly is swelling and the strange thing is, I have a feeling there's someone other than me inside, as if I'm beginning to be something and a half. It's doing that in my belly right now, here, touch."

I saw that I'd have to grab your hand, which you'd taken away from me, it was all soft and now I placed it on my belly and its surprises.

"At first it made a quiet buzzing, as if a baby bumblebee were travelling in my belly from right to left, drawing a line, very softly, very very softly, and I know what a baby bumblebee is. Can you feel it moving inside me right now? It's starting to be more like punches, like gentle whacks that the life deep in my belly is giving me. Every time that happens, no matter where I am or on what page or in what sentence, I write these words in my book of spells: and shoo. I much prefer these little punches of life I can feel inside me, shoo, shoo, to the blood I flick by the handful, I tell you, or the whacks of my late father."

Again, all this put in such a way that you'll think I'm cute and charming enough to drive a person crazy, but the inspector looked at me as if he couldn't understand how I could laugh at a time like this. And what was so special about this particular moment? Why should it leave us speechless more than any other? For mine was an innocuous laugh, you see, not like my brother's, it was more a bee's laugh, which is the most innocent thing on earth, because thinking about that vibration inside me put sweet thoughts into my noggin, and given the number of sweet things that come to me on this blasted planet I wasn't about to throw gobs of spit at it to ward off spells.

"Yesterday I could feel that you'd detached yourself from me because you'd felt that my belly was swollen. And you ran away crying: We mustn't! We mustn't."

We heard a shot. The shed window went flying and a giddy whistling sound passed over our heads.

"That monster is firing at us!"

A second detonation. This time the bullet must have got lost in the stones of the wall outside. The Fair had huddled into her little heap with a kind of moaning sound, her head tucked under her wing like a partridge. The inspector knelt down and ventured a look out the eviscerated window. I can't say what it did to me to see you on your knees like that, with just your face lit by the daylight falling from the window, how majestic I thought you were and all the rest, it was like joan of arc receiving a flash of the holy ghost inside her head, deep in her dungeon cell. Then you leaped at me and, in a whisper that sounded like a cry:

"He's out of ammunition, I think. He's gone to the house for more. Hurry! You mustn't stay here. We'll escape on my bike!"

We left at top speed. I fell in the mud as I was running towards the bike, for the book of spells is cumbersome and I didn't want to leave it behind, as you may well imagine. But you picked me up, my prince, you picked me up. You propped me against you, right against your belly, to make me safe from my brother's muskrat, and all at once it started to get warm and vibrate between my thighs, it felt good, and as your steed was backfiring I felt myself being swept away in a magnificent fit of exhilaration, with the gates open wide in the direction of your kingdom.

There were two more detonations, if my memory is reliable, which we could barely hear on account of the humming of your steed, then there was a third, a final one, and then, I don't know how I was able to see it, it was so quick, you brought your hand to the back of your neck the way a person does when a fly bites, and your steed lost its head, everything flipped over and my skull crashed into the ground, don't ask me how. When I could finally pull myself up, the wheels of the bike kept spinning in the air all by themselves, because it was lying on its side, and the noise it made, you'd have thought it was howling in despair. And I saw you on the ground nearby, your hand on your throat, I saw the blood spurt rhythmically between your fingers and I don't know how long it may have been before you stopped looking at me altogether with those eyes of a creature that doesn't understand why it's being struck with blows, at once surprised and pleading, then all at once frozen there like holes, but I laid my forehead on your chest and I cried, I cried.

When I finally lifted my head, I tell you, the steed had stopped howling and I had lost my innocence about all things. I had understood definitively that our dreams come down to earth just long enough to thumb their nose at us, leaving a taste on our tongues like blood-clot jam, and I picked up my book of spells just like that, in the middle of the field, and my pencil followed like the day the night, because a secretarious, a real one, never shrinks from the duty of giving a name to things, that's his role, and I thought I'd already been disarmed enough by life that I didn't wish to deprive myself further, in the manner of franciscans and soft-eyed mules, and to go so far as to divest myself of my dolls of ash, I mean words, so true is it that we are bereft of everything we know not how to name, as the Fair Punishment would put it, if she knew how to speak.

As for my brother, I can't deny it, he went on bustling about as if things were perfectly normal, as if they still made sense, that's because of his balls I think. Humph. Now and then I would glance at him, not scornfully but taking pity on him with his poor head charred by grace and all smeared with religion. A while ago he went away to dig a pit along the pine grove, that's done now. Then he came back and moved restlessly around the house. He took a knife and severed the cord that was wrapped around horse like a girth, so that he could grab hold of the sack containing papa's corpse, I'm well aware of it. And then I saw the first curls of smoke rising from the library, where my brother had been attending to I know not what no more than twenty minutes earlier. I bowed my head and went back to writing. At the point we're at now on this earth.

Hardly more than a few moments later I saw him approaching again, but this time he was approaching me. I can't say I was actually afraid because there's no longer much to keep me here below, where to put it bluntly everything is a chain, and existing no longer matters much once those chains are lost, the Fair wouldn't contradict me on that. If I still had any chain myself, it was the one inside, the one that had linked me to my belly for what would soon be more than two seasons. I thought to myself: As long as that one holds . . .

As for what brother could do to me now, humph, and I sent him packing with my eyes full of little thunderbolts. He did something with his arm that told me to go to hell, then he took a small piece of the universe that was flaccid and sticky out of his pocket and threw it in my face. I looked in the grass to see what it was. Oh my. Even our only toy the frog has reached the stage of mortal remains. Brother took off again, in the direction of papa's. And lugged them away with difficulty, because a body is heavy with no one inside it, and as promised he sank them to the bottom of the pit he'd just dug, then on top he planted the cross that I constructed yesterday in the morning. And that's that. All has been consumed.

Or so I thought. For whom do I see turning up behind me out of the blue with a smack of his cane on my back? That's right, the beggar. Ah la la. With his snickerings of depraved lust and the sounds from his throat like a dog, which as we know are his way of expressing himself. I still had my nose inside my book of spells, not far from the remains of my fiancé with his eyes staring like holes, and the beggar started tickling my ribs with the blasted tip of his cane. What have I done to the good lord, holy mother? He flattened himself on top of me, true as I'm standing here. I had his ugly mug in my face, and the powerfully musty smell of his food sandwich, some meatish filaments of it still hung from between his teeth. Grimacing, he started to pull at my eyelids and my lips the way papa made us do to him in the belle époque, you'd think it was to make fun of me and to get his own back. Finally he lifted my skirt and started trying to squirm on top of me like brother with his balls, so I cried out to ask for brother's help, but you can imagine. Kid brother had come back to the vicinity of horse, I could see him, and let me tell you, kid brother will roast in hell, if he hasn't already, because listen to what he did. He picked up his rifle, stuck it under the jaw of horse, who was half lying down, and made it blow up, bedlam! For one very brief moment I spied a bouquet of yellow, red, and blue smoke in a sheaf all around him, with a sound like hailstones. Horse collapsed like a sack. And that was the moment the sly devils chose to turn up at the end of the road, one big, tight-packed heap of neighbours who had come directly from the village, how typical.

Brother fired his rifle in their direction, by way of panic. Then, leaving his muskrat behind on what remained of defunct horse, he decamped the site at breakneck speed and shoo. And the beggar pulls up himself and his pants, fortunately before he could do the slightest damage to me, glory be to god for a favour granted, and there he was hurling himself onto his joystick, waving his arms at the sly devils, playing the innocent and acting as if he were happy as a demon to see them, wily to the core, the coyote. While I took advantage of the situation to speed away and hide in the vault with the Fair.

Who seemed to understand something about all the catastrophes that were happening to us: I told you there was some brightness in her bonnet. She was beside herself, meaning that she was swinging her heavy head very very slowly to the right and left while emitting a long, dreary, uninterrupted aaaaaaaaaah that just barely emerged from her throat. Only once before had I seen her in this state and it had been no laughing matter, it was the time papa was cutting her wrappings and he let the scissors slip so that a little bit of blade landed on her absent skin, and she started to make a dreary and uninterrupted aaaaaaaaaah like that while swinging her noggin right and left by way of pain, and papa cried, it gave him so much remorse in his chest, and for two minutes he kept gently and cautiously smacking kisses on the Fair Punishment's forehead. Through the window I was watching where the sly devils were, and the beggar in their midst, who was hopping on the spot and growing animated and playing the hero. There must have been a good dozen of them, I wouldn't take the trouble to count them, humph. One had been scraped on the thigh by my brother's rifle bullet, if I understood rightly, and he too was playing the hero, showing the others his thigh. They were looking towards the bookhouse, that's the pet name we gave it, yours truly's bookhouse, and wondering what to do about the fire, which was starting to catch the wind in its sails, and great puffs of reddish-brown smoke. There was some panicking and milling in circles among our neighbours. The curé was there too, the little priest from the day before who'd given me a taste of his earboxes and was now pretending to pray over the remains of what had once been a knight in armour as well as the great love of my life, and that gritted my teeth and knitted my brows a little, I'd gladly have given that soutane a kick in the inflations, but. In the end my brother came back of his own poor initiative and, let me tell you, it was out-and-out surrender. Kneeling at our neighbours' feet, with his shoulders on the ground and his hole in the air, he was protecting the back of his skull with both hands and shaking like the mint jelly we occasionally used to garnish the Fair's porridge, I know what I'm talking about. The officer from the day before, with the pistol of dizzying proportions, seemed to me to be talking softly to my brother, to avoid frightening his panic beyond the proper degree, and encouraging him to stand up, but as you can imagine, with his hole still in the air and his hands on the back of his skull there was nothing to be done. They had to kneel to snap on the handcuffs. Ah la la, if you want my opinion.

And there it is, everything draws to a close, it's a universal law, beginning with this book of spells, no more than another few pages before the grand sacrifice. I have very little time and I won't have had enough to recount everything, you can see that I'm at a loss. To the string of my disappointments I would just like to add this, namely that I've been wondering for a few scant seconds whether everything we've experienced since the morning of the day before, the failures, rages, panics, and humiliations we'd thought were completely outside any paternal orbit, as it's called, whether in fact all those things weren't exactly what papa would have wanted them to be. I fear we've done nothing but continue to obey him, without knowing it, unable to do otherwise, the two of us swept away by an inevitable movement that emanated from him and continued to drag us in its wake, forever and always. I'm saying it the way it appears to me. Maybe we've never stopped being his dolls of ash. I mean that from deep down in his death he was still toying with us, chuckling at our angelic noggins with the same worrisome assurance that I myself display by using words. Father was not a man whose power stops so short. Perhaps his own mortal remains were merely some plaything to delude us, ourselves as much as the universe in its pensive totality. I was thinking of this as I looked at the pit where brother had buried father's bombastic death next to the pine grove, and I told myself that if someday people started saying that something underneath this cross with no name or date could still, with hidden irony, stir the earth in one way or another however feebly, I wouldn't be surprised, you see. I mean that our neighbours tend to astound in the presence of whatever has disappeared nowhere, because of their human essence; it inclines them to ruminate on the grass of the dead, which makes them imaginative. And the first sun of any religion, if I'm not mistaken, is always a corpse that moves.

BUT NO THANK YOU, no more for me. I've lost interest in the sly devils' show and I've started to pack my bags with all my little belongings that lay scattered in the vault, beginning with the wooden plank, which I'll surely find time to talk about again, there'll be other opportunities before the last words rain down. I also took my favourite picture of my handsome cavalier and wedged it against my belly under my skirt, and an old dictionary of the memoirs of saint-simon that was falling into selected parts. From the Fair Punishment's expression as she watched it was easy to see she had some brightness, because she was no longer moving her noggin slowly to right and left, she was observing me intently as I packed my bags, and that placed some berefted mist in her eyes. But what can I say, are we put here, I mean on this blasted earth, to be sentimental?

I drew closer to the little heap of her and crouched down so she'd be within reach of my hands and my mouth. I smiled at her while I stroked her skull and pointed to the chain on the wall with a sad shrug of my shoulders, to make her understand that, all things considered, I'd rather bring her with me, but there was nothing to be done, blame it on impossibility. I even used words to tell her that in any case our neighbours would find her eventually, and perhaps a new life would begin for her then, with sunshine, outside her dungeon. Poor Fair Punishment, how she looked at me. Really, her eyes, I swear, they're a bubble to mine, it was as if I were looking at my own face in the well bucket in summertime. She started again with her long, dreary, uninterrupted sound, but I put my hand over her teeth, gently, with a smile and a look in my eyes, which were now laden not with little thunderbolts but with salty water that would have the good fortune of reassuring her, at least such was my prayer to heaven, if there still is one. As for the glass box, I said to myself, let the dead bury the dead, and I was gone, shoo, out the back door. The sly devils didn't see me.

Deep down, to be honest, I'd always known, in a way, that I was a slut, I didn't have to wait for a cavalier to call me a wild little goat before I suspected it. But my father had treated me as his son, and that had put a rod between my legs, figuratively speaking. I mean that I was forbidden to move around freely within myself, I was all boxed in, stifled, unable to proceed calmly towards my own simple truth, namely that just because I didn't have balls like you know who, it didn't make me abnormal in my future mortal remains or inside my noggin. Now, from there to having a little sister, that's some margin, as well as a small plank, which I'll say more about later. As for my brother, you'd have thought that he was the first person ever to have balls, and that he was discovering them with wonder for the first time every morning the good lord brings us, but jupiter junior has never worked out the connection to what the kitten kaboodle is for. There are things that never set foot inside his noggin, you see, and he was sincere, I believe, when he introduced his finger into papa's sensitive orifice just the day before, to see if it was possible that he and I had emerged from there, even when he saw the sausage arch its back through the power of magic, that was a big surprise for kid brother, he never would have expected that from the mortal remains of a defunct. For a long time I too thought papa had kneaded us out of mud, because of religion. But the things we believe through religion and the things we believe period are two different matters, and I'd been seeing since I was knee-high to a grasshopper how and from where calves and piglets arrived, and I never saw myself as an exception. The strong point is that kid brother too was well aware of what went on among those pensive creatures but I don't know, he never worked out the connection. What can I say, intelligence is like inflations, it's not something you can just decide to have. In any case, that's what was rolling around in my bonnet as I made my way, with no haste at all, towards the ballroom of my dreams, inhabited by the most amiable ghosts.

If I had time I'd have something to say about what the pigs in their wallow looked like, yike! Skin and bone, if that, and that's only the most affluent. And they trembled and they dripped a greenish liquid from their snouts, and then the cows and the sheep, if you can still call them that. We were a little negligent all the same, I confess. We'll burn for it somewhere, someday, I'm afraid, and when I get ideas like that, let me tell you, I don't give a fly's fart about the ethics of spinoza. It's no help whatsoever, and shoo. As for the stables, you'd need cannon just to open the doors. Tss. How dreadful. To say nothing of the hens.

And then, phoo, I stepped into the ballroom, climbing stairs that were like petrified clouds, because of the marble. I headed for the cupboards, like a gadfly going to the only flower in the garden, to stuff myself along the way with an orgy of light. With my little arms and my little legs I opened the tall, heavy glass doors that look out in all directions over the mirrored plain, and watch out for your dresses because I know you won't believe me but there was sunlight! A lot of sunlight, even, and it was falling over the countryside through a hole in the clouds. I took a long bath in it to console my heart. The mountain begins here and goes to the horizon, making leaps along the slight slopes and little jumps, and streams that you can hear hissing and falling. It was in that direction that papa let off the cannon shot on the days when the billy goat arrived. The spinach in the forests is slowly turning yellow and hot-pepper red as autumn sneaks up. Not the evergreens, of course, they don't even know what a season is, the sly devils. But the other trees, because there are some even here, leafy and tousled and as round as mushrooms. And I asked myself, what have we done with all that, thinking about ourselves as much as about our neighbours in their pensive totality. Sometimes you might think I'm the only one on this earth who loves it, life I mean. But if you try to love, everything becomes complicated, because not many people have the same imaginings of it inside their bonnets. Would there be enough room on the earth for each of us to take a little white pebble and mark every one of our disappointments in love, I tell you those pebbles would be visible from the moon, along with the chinking wall. Take my brother. I have no idea what love meant for him, aside from squirming on top of me, which filled me full of rage and desperation but, well, with the pillow over my head and get your ass over here little goat, endure, endure it, until finally when the sausage went soft I could start breathing with my lungs again. When my mortal remains disappear I may go to the blazing coals because of this, but I record it here in all honesty and simplicity, I don't think I love my brother any more at all. Too bad. Disappointed me too much, too often. He promised me this, he promised me that — to wash his feet, to stop drinking fine wine on the sly. As for my father, what can I tell you, someone who spent long hours holding his hand in yours while he cried in a vault . . . He never squirmed on top of me, in any case, which is all to his honour, I declare that to the face of the author of things, without shame or pity. The Fair too I was fond of, but that . . . Because of her silence, which gave me the gift of words.

Be that as it may, I was on the mirrored plain and the smell of burned wood was coming to me on gusts of wind because I tell you, the library was burning fiercely, all twisted in its smoking and flaming. The same for the portrait gallery. With the tip of one eye I could barely make out a neighbour or two, who at this distance could just as well have been flies on a dunghill and weren't worth much more, if I'm any judge. I think they were carrying buckets or something comparable, fools that they are, because with such a fire they might as well have tried to put it out with spit, that wouldn't have changed a hell of a lot if you want my opinion. As for the kitchen of our earthly abode, god knows I didn't give an owl's hoot about that. I was taking advantage of the bright sunshine to scribble to my heart's content, with the wind at my stern, my bow planted in the horizon, the page is a blank caravel, and I'd placed the small wooden plank under my book of spells, intending to make the connection between the two. I mean I wanted very much to talk about that plank in this book of spells, because I wanted, so to speak, to marry them together for the great sacrifice I'm preparing to commit.

I'm talking about the plank, which dates back to before I had any memory of whacks, if not longer, when there was sunshine all day long, and the little cherub next to me who was a bubble to me. Papa, who through the power of magic captured the rays of sunshine that ran aground in his magnificat glass, had written on the plank in letters of fire these words, which are there still, and though they may look like nothing they reverberate in my head like an oath: *Ariane and Alice, age 3*. Underneath there was a heart outlined in black soot, which was also drawn with concentrated thunderbolt, and from merely scribbling this the secretarious gets the impression that she can hear behind her the voice of that slut who smelled so fresh and pure, a grande dame, as the duc de saint-simon would have said, he still wrote in vulgate, and in my memory the laughter of that grande dame was like a star's reflection in a pool of virgin water.

After I'd written the preceding caravels I went back inside the ballroom. Having folded the wing of the grand camel, if that's what it's called, and then deposited the book of spells on top of it, along with the small wooden plank, I began to arrange my cutlery on the floor in rows under the glare of the chandeliers, which glittered in the sun like tsoulalas, for one mustn't let oneself be beaten down by trifles in this life, and I was ready to dance again, let the party begin!

But suddenly my belly let out a howl and there I was on my knees, as if I'd been gunned down, stunned and dazzled by an abrupt flash of pain. I felt as if someone had just torn my inner depths like cloth. And all around my skirt, what's this? A puddle of the nastiest jelly, with glimmers of water, don't ask me what hole that came from. Calm down, Alice. I got up. I walked like a heron on the fragility of my legs, stooping a little, my hand held to my belly of surprises with a kind of concerned tenderness that no one has ever shown me, but I was no longer all alone inside myself, I had someone to caress. For I was beginning to understand what was happening, you see, I didn't need to consult a dictionary, it was calves and piglets again. It wants to come out, but I'd never have thought it would want to come out so soon. Relying on what I'd gleaned here and there in the course of my reading, I had given myself three seasons, and it's true of course that we are approaching that number, I stopped bleeding for the first time when we were still in the snows of winter, as my recollections testify. Yet my belly isn't all that big, and that's what's bothering me now. Everything in nature's works confounds us, it seems that the author of all things enjoys this kind of game.

So it was with agony that I reached the grand camel,

where I'd put the book of spells. I stayed on my feet because merely bending my legs to sit down set off a scream in my depths. It was all the same to me, I would write standing up. In any case the pain had already calmed down a few minutes later, though the little goat felt strongly that she hadn't seen the last of it, that it would be back with others of its kind. In the meantime I would cope by scribbling, with my hand in the hand of patience. One does not escape oneself, in one sense or another, even through fear there's no escape. For even joy, especially joy, makes me afraid of myself, I don't know if I've made myself clear, and while I waited for life to explode in my body, for the true lacerations inside me to begin and for the child howling its name to demand its portion of this wreck of a planet, I took refuge in my pencil as is my wont. For what is there to do in this life but write for nothing? I know, I know, I said, "words: dolls of ash," but that too is misleading because some of them, when they're well ranked into sentences, give you a genuine shock when you come in contact with them, as if you were laying your palm on a cloud swollen with thunder at the very moment when it's about to let go. That's the only thing that helps me. To each his expedients.

FOR ABOUT HALF A TURN of the clock now, I've been writing while standing hunched over the grand camel's wing. The afternoon's last sunbeams are pouring onto the slabs beneath my feet in warm puddles, and I feel as if I'm standing in a stream up to my knees in sunlight. By dint of saying that I'm nearing the end, I intend to finish this blasted last will and testament. After that, if the tearing in my waters isn't too harsh, I'll make an out-and-out attempt to burn these pages in the same flame as the small wooden plank, and that's that. The camel's entrails will serve as the firebox, I can't wait to hear the music that wells up. I'll use the matches I brought from the vault, where papa always left some lying around, out of the Punishment's reach, of course, but where she could still see them as symbols, and remember them and draw a lesson from them, and feel remorse. And if any sly devil should stumble upon this book of spells he wouldn't understand a thing, because I write with just one letter, a cursive *l* it's called, I string them together page after page, caravel after caravel, nonstop. For I've finally done the same thing as my brother, what else is there, I've adopted his method of scribbling, the writing goes faster that way and it's the real reason I can't reread myself. But still, by lining up these cursive *l*s I can hear all the words inside my bonnet, and that's enough, it's no worse than talking to yourself. Besides, what difference does it make?

And so I shall immolate this book of spells, just as papa used to sacrifice the billy goat for the renewal of spring. I can see us again, all three of us, with fife and flipple flute and tambourine. At each return of the season when father punished jesus for dying forever yet again, we'd slay the billy goat, at least papa would, and he and brother would even dip into the fine wine by drinking a toast from its horns, ugh. I myself drank from the bottle, taking pity on the poor beast, on his splayed carcass that had been stripped to the viscera and opened like a dictionary, while those two guzzled the scarcely boiled innards. We drank till our skulls burst, bottles and flasks, starting with me, it had to be done, and horse too. Once he was drunk, Papa would stagger like a cursed monk with the flipple flute in his hole for heaven's sake, and, laughing all the way, he'd drag my brother by the leg and shut him inside the vault by force. Kid brother blubbered and bawled and screamed that he wanted to be let out at once and, the Punishment, what would you expect, it put her in a terrible state. But the alarm of my brother, who was pounding on the door from inside, ah la la, distraught and his health in a panic, you'd have thought it was a bird in a turpentine suit, I myself never laughed so hard, because of what fine wine does to our heads, against which we are powerless. But in my heart, without its showing, there were tears and weeping because of the Fair.

Be that as it may, my own billy goat will be this gospel of my hell which I shall burn along with the small wooden plank, that sacrifice will have the virtue of doing no harm to any beast, for the beasts are as immaculate as the palm of the clouds, which are innocent to the core. For I too find myself dreaming about renewal. I understand that a new existence, a springtime in autumn's midst, may be about to begin for me and I never should have let myself go, dreaming is risky for my self-assurance, which is fragile. It seems to me that I could live here with the child that will emerge in a few hours from my body. I can see that if I want, I can close my eyes, which are the eyes of the Fair, and see it as clearly as I can see my hand as it writes, with my lids open. We would form a big family, just the two of us alone. We would live so much together and so close to one another that a smile that began on my lips would end up on hers, for example. I would comb her little wings while we waited for them to moult. I would make her swaddling clothes of butterfly wings, and pillows of tenderness, with the love that was never given to me, any more in fact than it was given to the billy goat that we stunned with a stone while I danced around it with my tambourine, and no one would come and stick his dirty paws in our existence with his balls. We would nourish ourselves with the milk of goats, with the vegetables and grasses that are peace on earth, or with mushrooms that I'm acquainted with, we wouldn't spend our time murdering animals to gorge on their corpses when they've never done us any harm.

And we would live here in this ballroom, and in the towers too, and in whatever outbuildings we chose, because tell me, will you, what right has anyone to tear the countess of soissons away from this land that belongs to her through all the nooks and crannies of her fiery flesh?. . . I seem to be scooping up clouds, I know. But you can't blame any of that on impossibility. She would learn to read with me. From the dictionaries we'll fetch tomorrow from what's left of the charred library, where some, I dare believe, will have been spared — you wouldn't think so but dictionaries are tough, they have the calm obstinacy of the wood from which they're born, trees could give us no gifts more beautiful. And we'll read, we will read! Till we fall to the ground ecstatic because after all, what does it matter if stories tell lies as long as they stream with brightness, as long as they spangle with stars the bonnets of children who've tumbled from the moon and lie together side by side, two by two, she and I? I think I have a fever, my temples are oozing and throbbing like the flanks of a dying basset hound, if my opinion is still of any interest to you.

Yes, I say she, because this cherub will be like a bubble to me, I offer as proof the conviction I can feel inside my belly. She will grow up without ever knowing whacks, like the flowers, which don't have to be mistreated to grow with all their colours flying. She'll be attentive and polite to all animals, she won't abandon them to bereftment and hunger like some I know, alas, who will roast. I will teach her to beware of seductive and destructive manikins and dolls as if they were fire, for they are dangerous because of their beauty, according to the sayings of my father it's at the age of four that one is too fond of matches, and I'll call her Ariane in memory of the punishment . . .

A shudder of white cloth crosses the splendour of the autumn sky and drifts above the river, you might think it was a kite the size of a church, it's the snow geese. I had a kite once in the shape of a fish with golden scales, I looked after it because it was my cloud, but one day it slipped out of my fingers and flew away up above, I gazed at the wreck of it at the summit of a tree one summer long, that was when I was beginning to swell on my torso, troubles always arrive hand in hand. As for the snow geese, every year my father and I would go up to the summit of yours truly's bookhouse to watch them take off. This fall they seem to be early and I see that as a sign. They're like thoughts that are too sweet, too beautiful for us to keep cozily inside our chests in anticipation of the long winter months, we must resign ourselves to the fact that they leave us in one go, as a swarm, like those that rise up inside me when I think about the blessed fruit of my womb, thoughts that lure my heart and terrify me with joy and that I must drive away from my bosom, for already there's no time left for dreams of paradise, I can feel within me, from the dike that's about to burst, that soon I shall be in the grip of deliverance, and I know from experience that my imaginings have never brought me anything good, any more than my memories, in fact, and now I have less desire than ever to go mad like a flaming partridge stuck through my hat, all smeared with the blood of their religion, and to end up devastated from having waited too long here below, a martyr to hope, which can happen in the best of families.